Other Books by Patricia Apelt

*Circumstantial Connections*

# Green Mountain Mysteries and Ship Shadows

PATRICIA APELT

ARCHWAY
PUBLISHING

This is a work of fiction. All of the characters, names, incidents, organizations, and dialogue in this novel are either the products of the author's imagination or are used fictitiously.

Archway Publishing books may be ordered through booksellers or by contacting:

Archway Publishing
1663 Liberty Drive
Bloomington, IN 47403
www.archwaypublishing.com
1 (888) 242-5904

Because of the dynamic nature of the Internet, any web addresses or links contained in this book may have changed since publication and may no longer be valid. The views expressed in this work are solely those of the author and do not necessarily reflect the views of the publisher, and the publisher hereby disclaims any responsibility for them.

Any people depicted in stock imagery provided by Getty Images are models, and such images are being used for illustrative purposes only. Certain stock imagery © Getty Images.

ISBN: 978-1-4808-7403-9 (sc)
ISBN: 978-1-4808-7401-5 (hc)
ISBN: 978-1-4808-7402-2 (e)

Library of Congress Control Number: 2019902738

Print information available on the last page.

Archway Publishing rev. date: 3/19/2019

In loving memory
of two extraordinary ladies,
Mrs. Bonnie Ferreira and Mrs. Harriette Gorman.

# Acknowledgments

PECIAL THANKS TO MY SUPPORT team. Daughters Kathy Apelt, Wendy Apelt Matheson, and Laura Apelt Maney, and my other "Beta Readers" Patricia (Pat) Darby, Patricia (Pat) Green, Linda Hartmann, Joy Rezek, and Sally Stephens. Thanks also for the continued support of the males in my life, husband Walter and sons John and Charles. Also a special thanks to my "Technical Advisor" Ed Hartmann. Your critical comments, positive and negative, helped me prepare this work for publication.

Again, my thanks to William Curry, Gwen Ash and the rest of the team at Archway Publishing. As with the first book, your help and support were very much appreciated and made this sequel possible.

# Chapter One

"I'M COMING! I'M COMING!" KATIE Mayhew called from the bathroom. She knew her husband was as anxious to get to the meeting as she was. As a matter of fact, she was so excited about this meeting and hurrying so much, she was having a hard time getting ready. It seemed nothing was going right or quickly. With a final flick of her hairbrush, she ran into the bedroom, grabbed the sweater she had tossed on the foot of the bed earlier and continued on to meet Russel in the foyer of their home. He grabbed her hand, gave it a quick kiss, then led her onto the waiting elevator.

It was a short ride down--only two floors--but they took that time to give each other a hug and a more satisfying smooch, as Granny Edi called it. Still in their first months of marriage, they smooched often. At ground level, they hurried out to the car, where Katie's brother King and his wife Abbi were waiting for them.

Abbi enfolded Katie in a bear hug as she said, "I am so happy for you two!" Glancing at King, she added, "And us too! It's so wonderful of Granny Edi to do this for all of us. Come on, let's get going!"

They piled into King's rental car and buckled up. King

tooted the horn but even as he did, the other members of the family were stepping out of the back door of the dwelling next to their converted barn home and office. Each of them had big smiles and waved vigorously to those already moving toward the road leading into the village.

Sam and her husband Jeff climbed into the front of Jeff's car, while Melissa and her husband Will helped Granny Edi into the back, Will placing his hand over Granny's head as he helped her in. He then got in beside her and took her hand in his. They followed King and his passengers into the village but lost sight of them in the parking lot by the large building where their attorney had her office. Meeting again in the third-floor lobby, they all walked into the lawyer's office together, Will and Meli on either side of Granny Edi.

# Chapter Two

T HE PRETTY MIDDLE-AGED SECRETARY BEHIND the desk greeted them as they entered. "Hello, Aunt Edith. I'm Emily Dickson. It's good to see you again."

"Oh, hello, Emily! How are you? Has your daughter had her baby?"

"No, not yet. It's due next week."

Then she nodded and smiled at all of them and asked them to follow her. She led them down a short hallway and ushered them into a large room with a big table and a dozen chairs in the center.

"There's coffee, tea and a selection of pastries on the table by the window. Please help yourselves. I'll tell Miss Davis you are here."

As she went out, Sam and Melissa helped Edith into a chair at the table while Will went to the refreshment table.

"Do you want a glazed donut to go with your coffee, Granny?" he asked.

"Yes, please." she answered.

Walking back to the table he said, "Okay, here you go. Coffee at one o'clock, donut on a napkin at 6. There are also Danish pastries if you want one."

"Maybe later, thanks."

Telling Edith where her food was placed and putting a hand on her head as she was getting into a car were two of the few ways her family acknowledged her blindness. Having been blinded as a young woman, she had coped very well over the years and seldom needed extra help. The family did not give her lack of sight much thought anymore.

With Sam and Abbi choosing hot tea and the others grabbing a cup of coffee, they had all just settled around the table when the hall door opened.

A very attractive young woman walked in and went directly to Granny Edi. She leaned over to give the elderly lady a hug and said, "Good Morning, Aunt Edith! It's so good to see you again. I love the new yarns Mom has in her shop. She tells me that the yarn from your goats is one of her biggest sellers for Pins 'N Needles."

She then moved to the chair at the head of the table and put her armful of papers down.

As the young lady moved away, Granny Edi told her, "Thank you for the comment about the Melrose Farm yarns. Most of the credit goes to Russell and Molly Evan's grandson, Jared. Although, we will have to hire someone else now that school is beginning. As you know Jared teaches at the high school, and Russell is getting too busy with his construction company to care for the goats, chickens, and horses anymore. If you hear of anyone wanting a part-time job, please let us know."

"I'll do that." Turning to the rest of the group she said, "For those of you who do not know me, I am Jessica Davis, a junior partner here at Kendrick, Kendrick, and Meyers. Most people call me Jessie, and I hope you will too. Now, before we begin with all this paperwork, I would like to refresh my memory with what is actually happening here today. Like the rest of the village, Aunt Edith, I call you that even though we don't have any blood ties. As I understand it, that is pretty much what this meeting is all about."

Granny Edi spoke up to say, "Yes, I want to work out the paperwork necessary to gift all of my grandchildren, adopted or otherwise, with a part of their inheritance now, even if there is no real family connection."

"Of course." Jessie said. "Will, I have known you since we were in first grade, and I know you are really Aunt Edith's grandson since your mother was her daughter, Eve. Russell, I remember when you came to town almost five years ago and went to work helping care for Melrose Farm. The rest of you, I don't know quite so well even though I've seen you around the village from time to time. Could you please take turns telling me a little about yourselves, and exactly how you are tied into the group so I can better understand what Aunt Edith wants? Samantha, since I have been told you were the first on the scene after Russell, why don't we start with you?"

Sam sat up a little straighter in her chair, cleared her throat, and began. "After suddenly quitting my job at an advertising agency, I was starting on a vacation to clear my head when I ran into a very heavy wind and rain storm. It was late at night, and I couldn't see very well through all the rain, so I turned into what I thought was a state road, only to learn later it was Granny Edi's driveway. When that driveway collapsed because of all the rain, my car slid down and got stuck in her ditch overnight. I found her the next morning while searching for my cat, who had escaped from my car through a broken window. Granny Edi was under her kitchen table, where she had fallen when a tree crashed into her kitchen during the storm. She had a broken leg as a result of that fall and hired me as a companion to help her while the leg healed. I have been with her ever since. Abbi, you were the next to arrive, so I'll turn it over to you."

"Okay." Abbi looked around at the others. When they all gave her an encouraging smile, she took a deep breath, looked directly at Jessie and said, "I also was on the move, but it was no vacation. I was in the process of running away from an abusive husband. I had packed up everything that was mine, including my horse, Blaze. I was trying to get as far away as possible when I found out Blaze needed to have several days outside the horse trailer because of a swollen leg. I was sent to Melrose Farm to ask if I could rent space in the pasture. Not only did I receive a warm welcome, when Granny Edi found out I was pregnant, she insisted I stay there until after the baby was born. So I did."

Jessie interrupted to say, "I understand you had twins instead of just the one you were expecting!"

"That's right. A daughter, Larona Edith and a son, Lauren James. We call them Rona and Ren." Abbi explained. Then she looked around the table and said, "Next?"

"Hello again, Jessie. " Jeff took up the summary. "Doc Simmons introduced us last month at the business owner's meeting. I also happen to be Abbi's half-brother. I came looking for her after she ran away. Not knowing how long it would take, I had given up my practice to look for Abbi, so when Doc Simmons offered me a job at the hospital here in the village, I took it. I am now married to Sam, so this is my home. Who's next?"

"I guess that might be me." Melissa spoke up to say. "Sam and I roomed together in college and shared an apartment afterward. I am a photojournalist and was on an assignment out west when I was involved in a very serious automobile accident and lost both my sight and my memory." Waving her hand in the direction of the two sitting directly across from her, she continued. "King found me after the wreck and he and his sister Katie took care of me until Sam learned where I was and came for me. She brought me back here, I was accepted as part of the group, and ended up marrying Will. Katie? King? Either of you want to take over now?"

"Please excuse the interruption," Jessie said, "but Will, I have a question. From what my Mother told me, you were somehow involved in that accident of Melissa's. Is that correct?"

"Yes, but only slightly. Not so much her accident but in the events that lead up to it. As you know, I am an archeologist. I was at the base camp for my dig when my assistant turned on me, planning to steal the artifacts. He and his buddies were shooting at my workers. Melissa heard the shots, thought it was a movie being filmed, so stopped to take pictures. They started aiming at her, actually hitting her arm, so she ran to her camper and left in a hurry. I understand she ran into a heavy rainstorm and could not see well through the windshield they had broken while shooting at her. Trying to steer with one arm, she hit a boulder, blew a tire, ran off the road and tumbled down a deep gully. I could do nothing to help as I was being kidnapped at gunpoint. After a horrible trip locked in the back of a big truck with the stolen artifacts, I ended up locked in the hold of a ship. So I was never in a position to offer her any help."

"Mercy, that must have been very frightening for you, Melissa." Jessie said as she reached over to place her hand on Melissa's arm.

"I suppose it was, but I didn't remember that part until much later. When I was thrown out of my camper, I hit my head on a rock and ended up with amnesia. King, please take over. I don't want to think about that anymore."

"Understood, Sis." Turning to Jessie he continued.

"First, for your legal documents, Jessie, my name is actually Sebastian James. Since my last name is Cole, as in 'Ole King Cole', 'King' is a childhood nickname that still sticks. As for my relationship with the family, Will and I went to college together. I used to visit him and Granny Edi often during those years. When he found out that Meli had been near my home when she had that accident, he called me to see if I had heard about it and might know where she was. Katie and I brought Sam and Mellissa back here, I fell in love with Abbi, married her three days before the babies were born, and took her and the twins back to Texas with me. Katie, it's all yours."

Katie reached over to take Russell's hand. For courage or just to hold his hand, she didn't know or care. "I am King's sister so was around to help take care of Melissa until Sam showed up. I got to know Meli pretty well while she was staying in Texas with us so when King brought her home, I tagged along. After a couple of visits, Russell offered me the position of bookkeeper for his new construction business. Soon after that, he offered me the position of his wife. I jumped at the chance for both, so now I am a part of this 'no-blood-ties' family."

# Chapter Three

E DITH TURNED TO JESSIE AND said, "So you see, my dear, we are all connected through various circumstances and now these youngsters think of each other as brothers and sisters. Therefore, I like to think they are all my grandchildren. That is why we are visiting with you today. I would like to divide the farm into three equal sections, one-third for Katie and Russell, one-third for my Will and his Melissa, and one-third for Sam and Jeff. I also want to set up a trust fund for Abbi and King's twins."

"Well, Aunt Edith, as your attorney, I feel I must ask you if you are absolutely sure you want to do this."

"My William and I have discussed it at length. If we don't make these changes, he inherits it all and he says he doesn't want it. He does not want to be a farmer. If he says the papers are correct, I'll be happy to sign whatever you have drawn up."

"Okay, then." Jessie pulled her stack of papers over and picked up the top several. "By law, I am also obligated to tell you that in order for the visually challenged to sign legal documents, I should read all these documents to you out loud. However, since you said you are comfortable with Will telling you about what you are signing, we can skip that part.

"Thanks to Russell's call a couple of days ago, we were able to get the paperwork put together right away. Mr. and Mrs. Cole, the trust for your children is already set up, since that was the easiest to do. If you will both please read these documents, making sure all names are spelled correctly. When you finish, please sign on each line that is highlighted. When you are finished, please hand them to Will to go over for Aunt Edith's signature. Will, since you are sitting next to her, could you please guide her hand to the correct spot?" To the rest of them she added, "How about another donut or cup of coffee while they do that?"

All but Abbi, King, Will, and Granny Edi pushed their chairs back and went to the refreshment table, where they got refills and stood to chat a few minutes.

When Jessie noticed all the papers had been signed, she motioned the others back to their seats. Bringing refills for the four still seated, they took their places around the table and focused their attention on Jessie once more.

"As for the rest of you," she stated, "the division of property is outlined in the next few documents. Of course, we will have to wait until the surveys come back with the legal descriptions before we can have you sign the final papers, but these will get the ball rolling through the system.

"Will, you and Melissa shall retain full ownership of the central section, with Aunt Edith having a life right in that property. Mr. and Mrs. Mayhew, you will have a deeded ownership in the property where the barn and pasture are located. There will be one legal boundary to run along the common wall between your converted barn/ office/home and Will's farmhouse. This will extend in a straight line to the back of the property, turning to go across the back, up and over the mountain, then turning again to form the lot-line on the far side of The pasture out to the road. By the way, I would love to see what you have done to that beautiful old barn. I talked briefly with Jared Evans last week and he tells me it is wonderful."

Katie interrupted to say, "I've been told that it was a lovely barn to begin with, but that was before I came to live here. I visited once in awhile when King came to stay with his college buddy and brought me along but I never paid any attention to old barns back then. But now I think it is still beautiful and I am very happy it is now my home as well as where I work. Russell has done a marvelous job of converting it. Please, come over sometime and I'd love to show it off. I like to brag on his work!"

As they all chuckled, Jessie continued. "Dr. and Mrs. Barlow, you will have a deeded ownership in the remaining third of the property. Roughly, a long rectangle from the road at the front of the property, to include the mountain at the back, then across the back to meet with Will's property line, and then back to the road. As I said, the surveyors will have more precise measurements once they complete their work. Just sign these preliminary papers, then I can get the survey team started right away."

Papers were quickly read over, signed, passed around, signed again, then handed back to Jessie. "Now, are there questions about any of this?" Looking around the table all she saw were smiles and a lot of hugs from the ladies and back-slapping from the guys.

"I must say, you all seem to get along better than some 'real' families I have dealt with."

Granny Edi said, "Yes, I feel so blessed to have these young people around me. They truly are my 'real' family."

Will asked, "Do you need anything else from us right now, Jessie? If not, please join us for a celebratory lunch over at Rosie's Place."

"Why thank you Will, but I will have to decline your kind offer. I have your paperwork to finish up, the surveyors to contact, and two briefs for other cases to write. I'm afraid the rest of my day is going to be very busy with legal matters."

They all said their goodbyes with a round of handshakes, then left the office, waving to Mrs. Dickson as they passed her desk.

# Chapter Four

THEY LEFT THEIR CARS IN the parking lot and walked the short distance to Rosie's Place. She was waiting at the door with a big smile, having been expecting them. Will greeted her with a bear-hug and told her, "It's almost done, Aunt Rose. I am just about free of all that land! And, it is going to some of the best people in the world. Do you have time to sit with us?"

"Yes, I told my staff that I am taking off for a couple of hours to be with you. We have a big table saved over there on the left. Wait! I see Doc Simmons headed this way. Since he is your brother-in-law Edith, I knew he would want to come to the party. Hope you don't mind my inviting him."

"Not at all. I'm used to that old scalawag butting in."

Having just stepped into the diner and hearing their conversation, Doc Simmons defended himself. "Now, just a minute. I resent being called a scalawag! And I don't butt in. I just show up often."

Rose Green gave him a playful fist to his shoulder and turned him toward the table.

As the others moved toward their seats she spoke quietly to Granny. "So, Edith, are you still okay with all this? I know at one time you were hoping my brother and your Eve would take over the farm, but that did not work out because of their untimely deaths. Now, Will doesn't want to be a farmer either. This must have been a hard decision for you."

"Not really so hard after I finally realized Will was serious about not wanting to farm the place. I think I knew that even way back just after his parents were killed. He never had much interest in Melrose Farm, other than it was his home and he was happy to live there. As far as being a farmer, well, he always had other interests. I really think this division of the property is the best thing that could happen."

By that time, they had reached the table, so the subject was dropped. They concentrated on enjoying the pleasure of being together for another hour.

Back at the farm Russell quickly changed out of his suit, then went out to one of his construction sites. Katie didn't have to change since what she had on would be fine for her job as the bookkeeper in the Mayhew Construction office, just downstairs from her new home in what used to be the loft of the barn.

At the farmhouse, the others grabbed a cup of coffee and settled into the family room for a chat. Abbi and King had to leave soon to fly back to Texas, so could stay only long enough to collect the twins from Molly Evans, who had been watching them all morning. Then they left for the airport so King could fly them home in the corporate jet he had purchased for the joint Mayhew-Cole Construction Company. The plane did double duty as a way for him and his family to visit often.

They planned to stop on the way so Abbi could interview the potential new manager for the Phoenix Fabrics Mill that she and Sam had started. If all went well with that, they could start producing fabrics within the month. She was looking forward to having her very own fabrics to use for her costuming business. Sewing pre-Civil War costumes was a fun hobby for her, but finding the right fabrics for the time period had become a challenge. Sam had thought of buying a small mill and making their own fabrics. She was now doing the design work for the period costume fabric, while Abbi made the costumes for Riverboat shows, Plantation tour guides, and costumed parties. Buying the mill from her previous supplier had been a wise choice, but now she was anxious to actually get started with the production process.

Soon after the Coles were gone, Sam left to go out to her art studio to write up a new proposal for her latest client, and Jeff went to the hospital to check on a patient. When Granny Edi started nodding off for her afternoon nap, Will and Melissa tip-toed out to go work on the books each were writing.

# Chapter Five

T HINGS SETTLED INTO THE NORMAL routine after that, and it was almost three weeks later when Katie looked up from her account books to see a man walk into the Mayhew Construction office. Rapidly trying to remember if Russell had told her about a new client coming in, she stood and greeted him with her usual calm manner.

"Hello, welcome to Mayhew Construction. Please make yourself comfortable while I page Mr. Mayhew. May I tell him who has arrived?"

The man just stood there and looked at her, which was rather odd. And a bit frightening, since he was in a full-dress State Police uniform. She didn't think she or Russell had any reason to be visited by the police, but one never knew what these guys wanted. Selling tickets to the annual Policeman's Ball? Collecting for their Widow's and Orphan's Fund? A parking ticket she had forgotten?

Finally, the officer shook his head, then said, "I'm sorry. You lost me for a minute there, talking about paging Mr. Mayhew. I'm not here to see him. I was told to ask for Katie from Katie's Kennels. Do you know where I might find her?"

Katie took a deep breath, just then realizing she had not breathed normally while he stared at her.

"Why, yes. You are speaking to her. How may I help you?"

Extending his hand, he said, "My name is Jacob Finnigan. I work for a special unit in the State Police Force. A buddy of mine out in Texas told me he and his wife bought a puppy from you a while back. The dog was purchased as a Companion Dog for their son Billy, who is confined to a wheelchair."

Katie interrupted, "Oh, Mr. and Mrs. Roberts! Is Billy okay? Is the dog working out all right? They seemed a good match..."

Jacob held up his hand and assured her everything was good. "As a matter of fact, that's why I am here. They are so enthusiastic about that dog and the way he has helped Billy they insisted I come to you with my request."

"Well, I am so glad Copper is working out for them. Do you also need a Companion Dog?"

"No, my need is for something entirely different. Before I get into that, I guess I should find out if you even have any puppies for sale right now? The need is rather urgent, you see."

"Yes, I have four that could leave their mother anytime, but I like to train them with the new owner for a couple of weeks before I turn them over completely. What is so urgent that they would not have that extra training time?"

"Oh, they would get extra training time alright! Lots of

it. With me. You see, I head up the Search and Rescue Unit for my division, and a couple of our dogs are getting a little too old for this line of work. My buddy seemed to think your golden retrievers would be great replacement dogs. The urgency is that they do need a lot of training and I wanted to get started on that long before we have to retire the current dogs."

"Search and Rescue? I've never had one of my dogs go into that before. What would be required of them?"

"Well, first, the basic commands of course; sit, stay, come, etc. After those are second nature to them, we get into the nitty-gritty of how to go out and find someone who is lost, or how to sniff out drugs or weapons. Depending on the dog, that can take weeks or even months. A cadaver dog takes even longer."

"Cadaver dog?"

"One that is specially trained to find victims of collapsed buildings or caves or drowning."

"Oh. Dead people."

"Yes. Not pleasant to think of, I know, but the families of these victims thank us for it."

"Yes, I can understand that. How do you decide which type of training each dog will be best suited for?"

"We usually give all of them the same training at first, then let them show us what they like to do best. Most will have a preference for either drugs or people. There are even some that will be better suited to sniffing out weapons. It's part of my job to sort them out and see that each of them are trained for what suits them best."

"I see. I have noticed with my own dogs that some learn the different tasks much easier than others, even when they are from the same litter. Come with me and I will show you the heart of Katie's Kennel."

She led him through a door into what was the still the unmodernized section of the old barn, the other end having been turned into the offices for Mayhew Construction. Here, four horses, the herd of Granny's twenty Cashmere Goats, a couple of dozen chickens, several barn cats and Katie's golden retriever dogs lived in what had once been home to dairy cows when Granny Edi was a young girl.

# Chapter Six

KATIE HAD TO CALL FOR the dogs, since they were all outside in the fenced yard Russell and Will had put up for them behind the stalls where they slept.

Jacob looked around and stated, "It looks like you have made good use of the space here, but where are all the animals?"

"Oh, they all stay outside as much as they can during the day. Unless the weather is really bad, the goats and horses roam all over the pasture, the chickens and cats go wherever they wish, and my dogs stay in their own backyard. Unless I call them in to train or to show them off like I just did. And here they come! Hello, girls and boys. How're my babies? Okay now, be nice. Sit. Stay.

"From left to right, please say 'Hello' to Mattie and Rusty, the mother and father of this brood. Then in order this is Red, Lady, Jinx, and Lucky. Boy, girl, boy, boy. There were two others in this litter, but I have already placed them with their new owners. They come back each week to get further training based on their owner's needs."

"Beautiful dogs! I can see you take good care of them, so they are sure to be healthy." Jacob seemed very impressed with what he saw and continued. "Could we take them outside one at a time and see how they respond to commands?"

"Sure. Let's start with Lucky, shall we?"

"Whatever you think best."

"Lucky, heel." Once Lucky had come to sit by Katie's left foot, she waved her hand to the others, and said "kennel". They immediately got up and went back outside. Then Katie gestured toward a large open door at the far end of the barn.

"Out here is where I train them, so Lucky should feel right at home." Katie said, as she led the way outside and into the pasture out of sight of the rest of the dogs. She continued, "Lucky seems to be the least responsive of the four puppies. If he will do what you want, the other three should also, so this way you can save some time today. You will not have to test the others."

"Great! Will you show me what you have already taught him?"

"Love to."

Katie and Lucky went through a twenty-minute routine of commands and responses that were the beginning phase of what a Companion Dog needed to know.

When they finished and Katie had praised Lucky for his efforts, she turned to Jacob.

"Is there something else you would like to have him try? He should be willing to listen to your commands if I tell him to."

Jacob said, "Yes, there is one thing that I start my training sessions with. Let's see if he can pick up on it."

With that, Jacob pulled a white towel out of his pants pocket, and proceeded to engage Lucky in a tug of war.

After they had played for a few minutes, he turned to Katie and asked her to walk Lucky back into the barn until he called for them. When they were out of sight, Jacob pulled the towel over the ground several feet, then hid it behind a rain barrel at the corner of the barn. When he called them back, Jacob told Lucky to heel, then said "Find". Lucky looked up as if to say 'What?'. Jacob then said 'Find' again, adding hand signals as if he were pulling on the end of the towel. Lucky then stood up, looked around, then looked up at Katie to tell him what he should do, then sat back down. Jacob said sharply, "Lucky!" When he was sure of the dog's attention, he again told him to 'Find' and used the hand motions of the tug of war. Lucky looked around as if expecting to see the towel, then put his nose to the ground. He soon found the scent of the towel, followed it to the rain barrel and pulled out the towel. He pranced back to Jacob with his tail wagging.

"My God! Pardon me, Mrs. Mayhew! You said he was the least responsive, but he just picked up on the first stage of drug-sniffing on the third try. If your other two males are half as quick, I will purchase all three of them today."

Katie stood with her mouth open for a moment.

Then she said, "Why that would be wonderful, but I have several questions. Goldens' are not known for their scenting ability like rabbit hounds or other hunting dogs. What they do is based more on their keen intelligence and a good memory. How can you train them to use their nose? What you did with the towel was just playing. How can that be training for drug-sniffing?"

"Good questions, and I can answer both with one explanation. To us, it was just playing. But, as I said, it is the first step in the training. We play with the same towel every time, which smells a little like whatever laundry soap it was last washed in. This can go on for several weeks, depending on how long it takes the dog to find it quickly from different locations. Then we switch to special towels that have been washed in a solution that leaves no scent. Using gloves, we tie up a handful of drugs into the towel, so the dog begins to associate the scent of the drugs with his play toy. Soon, he is not trying to find his toy, but the drugs, because they are one and the same to him, and the drugs have a stronger scent than the towel, so it is easier to find. Then he learns to look for just the drugs because he knows once he has found them, he will get to play with his trainer. That is his reward for a job well done. Just as you praised Lucky and gave him a treat earlier."

"Amazing! But I have one more question. Why are you only interested in the males?"

Jacob smiled and said, "Don't think we aren't interested

in the females. We are, but for different jobs. Right now I only need drug sniffers and males seems to be better at that. Another officer handles the dogs that do the search and rescue work, which the females are better for, maybe because of the 'mothering instinct'. They want to find their puppies. That officer may be on the lookout for another dog, and I will certainly tell him about your Lady."

"Thank you! This is fascinating, and something I never thought much about before now. I wonder if maybe I might be able to watch my dogs work with you? I mean your dogs now, I guess. I mean when you start training these dogs." Katie seemed a bit flustered by the way things were moving so fast.

Jacob again smiled and said, "I think that can be arranged. I'll give you a check now for half the total amount. Then I would like to leave them with you for about two weeks while we make room for them at the department kennels. We can then come with a truck to pick them up and I'll give you the balance then. Does this meet with your approval?"

"Yes, that sounds about right. That will also give me time to get used to the idea of losing them. I love to see my dogs go to a good home, but it is always tough to say goodbye. This will be a different kind of home than I am used to finding for them, but maybe at least one of them can make a difference in our world by serving in this way."

"I'm quite sure at least one of them will. Judging by what I have seen today, I have high hopes for these guys."

Katie smiled and said. "Well, I always ask for their best and usually get it, so there should be no problem. I think my boys will do just fine."

"All right then. I left my briefcase in your office, so if we can go back there, I'll write out that check, and let you get back to Mayhew Construction business."

Katie called Lucky, told him 'kennel' and he was waiting at the gate to his 'backyard' when she and Jacob walked back into the barn.

# Chapter Seven

T HAT EVENING AS THE FAMILY gathered for their usual after-dinner talk in the family room, Katie was bubbling over with her news. Everyone was excited for her and the new direction the goldens were about to take. Jeff told them that he was seeing more young people admitted into the hospital with drug-related issues, and was glad to know that the State Police were doing all they could to stop the stuff from getting on the street.

He then turned to Katie and said, "Hey, Sis. With the sale of three, possibly four dogs all at one time, will you finally have enough money to buy that car you have been wanting?"

"Oh, my! I hadn't even thought about what to do with the money. But that is a good idea, Jeff. How about it, Sam? Can we go together? Remember, we talked about going car shopping soon, and you really do need a replacement for the one you have now."

Sam frowned at her husband and then told Katie, "Yes, I suppose I really do need to do that. Jeff keeps telling me I need to give up on my little car. I just hate to think about it, since it is the first one I ever had. I bought it used, the day after I graduated from college and it has served me well all this time. But I guess I can't expect the poor old thing to last forever."

Jeff laughed and said, "Old being the operative word there, love. What is it, seventeen now? Almost old enough to vote!"

Sam gave him a playful punch on the arm, then she and Katie made plans to go car shopping very soon.

During a pause in their conversation, Russell spoke up. "Umm...I guess I really don't have to ask permission anymore, thanks to your wonderful gift, Granny Edi, but I would like to make some changes to the barn. Well, not to the barn itself, but the pasture around it. Would that be alright with you?"

"My boy, I have given that land to you and Katie. We have all gotten the new deeds, so you are free to do whatever you want with it. But just out of curiosity, what do you want to change?"

"There is a problem every time I try to drive my truck into the pasture from the driveway on the far side. If you remember, Granny Edi, when I first brought my truck here, you told me I could use the driveway on this side and put it into the garage. Since Katie and I now live in what was the loft of the barn, it just seems to me that we should have our own driveway and garage on the other side. And now that Katie will be getting her own car, it is even more important, since the garage here is only big enough for two cars."

Granny Edi said, "Well that seems reasonable. But what is the problem you spoke of?"

Russell laughed then said, "You know how I told you the guy that delivers the shavings for the stalls for the goats and horses is always complaining about them getting in his way?"

When she chuckled and shook her head, he continued.

"Well now, it is even worse. With the horses, goats, chickens and sometimes even the cats always wandering around the door or close by, it is almost impossible to get into the pasture far enough to even get my truck off the road out front!"

As everyone laughed, he held up his hand. "Don't laugh! I was dodging around Star yesterday and almost hit one of the goats that ran between her legs. What I would like to do is fence off that area and build a new barn for the horses and goats a little further back, behind that new fence. I can then use the old barn as a garage for Katie and me, shared with her dogs, of course. The chickens and cats will continue to go where they like, but maybe they will learn to stay in the new barn too. Comments? Suggestions?"

Will spoke up. "Yeah, I have a few suggestions. First, I think this should be a joint venture. What I mean is let's build one new barn, but back it up to the line between us, with two doors, one on each side of the property line. That way, all of us on this side of the pasture fence can get to the horses easier when we want to ride. Also, we can let the horses out into the pasture on your side, but let the goats out on this side. I would like for them to get rid of all the weeds that have taken over since I last bush-hogged the place four years ago."

"Surely it hasn't been that long, Will." Granny Edi broke in to say.

"I'm afraid so, Granny. Remember, I did it just before I left to go on that last dig. With the initial planning for that, getting the crew together, working the site, and then my kidnapping with everything that entailed, it has been a good four years."

At the nod of agreement from her, Will continued. "After the land is cleared of weeds, we can over-plant with good grass and both the goats and the horses can graze on both sides alternately. That way, one pasture will not get over-grazed in any one season. I've had some of the farmer thinking come out in me lately, even though I said I did not want to be one. I took a close look at the pasture last week and noticed it seemed to be getting a little bare in places, so this will help with that."

"Sounds like a good plan to me. When do we start on this project?" Jeff asked.

Russell answered, "I would like to put up the fence, with a gate at the front, as soon as possible. The gate can be opened to let the animals into the old barn at night. I'm just afraid one of them could get hurt if we don't act quickly. After that, the new barn can wait until I have a crew between jobs. With my crews working on my own projects whenever I don't have something else for them to do, it will keep you guys from taking time away from your jobs and keep my people employed as well."

Soon after that discussion, everyone started yawning and left to go to bed.

# Chapter Eight

N EAR THE END OF TWO weeks, Jacob Finnigan called to make arrangements for picking up Katie's dogs. When he came with the truck, he had another man with him.

"Hello, Mrs. Mayhew. This is Brad Phillips. Brad runs the department that handles Search and Rescue. As it happens, he is looking for another dog for his team. Would you mind showing him your Lady?"

"I would be happy to. Right this way, Mr. Phillips."

Entering the barn, Katie called out to Lady. She came running in from the outside pen and immediately heeled at Katie's side without being told.

"Well!" exclaimed Mr. Phillips. "I am impressed already. What else has she learned under your tutelage?"

"So far just the usual basic commands one teaches a new puppy, but she is a very quick learner. How would you begin teaching her what she needs to know for Search and Rescue?"

Mr. Phillips smiled and asked, "Is there a place outside where we can go without distractions from other animals or people?"

Katie thought for a minute, then said, "Probably the

best place at this time of day would be on the other side of the farmhouse. Please follow me." Katie slapped her thigh once, which was Lady's cue to follow her, and led Mr. Phillips out of the barn, walked past the front porch of the farmhouse, and gestured to the yard beyond.

Mr. Phillips said, "Will she take commands from me this early?"

"If I tell her to listen to you, she should. If you take her around the yard and give her the simple commands first, she will get used to you pretty quickly."

"Alright. While we do that, will you please go find someone else in the family, tell them to stay where they are, but give you something of theirs to bring back here. A handkerchief, a shoe, even the book they are reading. Lady and I will wait right here for you."

Katie found Sam pulling weeds from the small flower bed by the back door. She told Sam what she needed, took the gardening gloves Sam offered and went back to where Lady and Mr. Phillips were still getting acquainted.

"Excellent!" Mr. Phillips said when he saw what she had. He took the gloves from her, asked the name of who they belonged to, then kneeled down and said Lady's name. When he was sure of her attention, he held the gloves under her nose so she could get a good sniff.

"Find Sam, Lady. Go find." Mr. Phillips again held the gloves to Lady's nose and repeated the command. Lady wagged her tail when she heard Sam's name, but made no other move.

Katie's shoulders slumped, thinking Lady had failed her first test.

Mr. Phillips saw her disappointed look and said, "Wait a few minutes before you think she is a failure. Come on Lady, let's try again." Once more, he held the gloves out to Lady and repeated, "Find Sam. Where is Sam?"

At that, Lady lifted her nose, took a sniff or two, and started running toward the back of the house.

Katie and Mr. Phillips followed her at a lope to find Lady had not only found Sam but had also bowled her over and was busily licking her face.

Mr. Phillips looked at Katie and said, "Well, it looks like Lady passed with flying colors. I think she will be a great addition to my team."

Both Katie and Sam were grinning broadly when Jacob Finnigan came around the corner of the house.

"Hey, Brad! There you are. I wondered where you went."

"Right here getting to know my new dog! I think Lady and I are going to form a good team."

"Ah! I thought you might feel that way." Turning to Katie, he said, "What I didn't tell you, Mrs. Mayhew, is that Brad was looking for a new partner for himself. He will be the one to train her, she will live in his home with his family, and they will be on call when someone gets lost. This is much like the homes you find for all your dogs, right?"

"Right! I'm glad she has found a loving home. What about my guys? Will they live in a kennel all the time??"

"Nope!" Jacob said with a smile. "All three of them will go to our main facility first, where they will be evaluated as to which path we want to lead them, then they will be matched with a human partner just like Lady. Their partners, male or female, will be a person that bonds with them quickly, just like you try to find the right match for your Companion Dogs."

"Oh, I feel so much better about selling them to you now. I know these types of dogs are needed, but I get very possessive of the pups I raise, and I'm concerned about their lives once I've said goodbye to them. It sounds like I need not worry about these four being well loved."

"No worries on that score! All of our teams are very devoted to each other. Now, Brad, I have the three guys all loaded into the truck kennels, and we are ready to head out. Have you settled up with Mrs. Mayhew yet?"

As he whipped out his checkbook, Brad said, "No, but that will not take long. If you could escort my Lady to the last kennel on the truck, I won't be but a minute."

As he was saying this, he was looking at Jacob with a question in his eyes. Jacob had been staring at Sam rather strangely. Noticing Brad's look, Jacob gave him a negative shake of his head, indicated that he would explain later, and went to put Lady into the truck.

When all of them had walked around to where the

truck was parked, Katie went to say a final goodbye to her babies while the others stood to the side and chatted.

Jacob spoke up to say to Sam, "Excuse me, but we have not met formally. I am Jacob Finnigan."

"Oh, sorry. We got so involved with the dogs, we did not follow the usual introductions. I am Samantha Matthews Barlow. So glad to meet you. I know Katie has been worrying about what happens to her dogs once they leave here, but I think you and Mr. Phillips have put her mind to rest."

"I have told her she will be welcome to come out to watch their training. Please feel free to come with her if you wish."

"Thank you. I just may do that."

"Do what, Sam?" Katie said as she walked up to them.

"Go with you when you visit the training sessions."

"Yes, when would be a good time to do that, Mr. Finnigan?"

"I'll give you a call when we have them all settled in and comfortable with their partners. Right now, we need to get going. I don't like to leave them in the truck any longer than necessary."

"Then 'Bye for now, and I'll look forward to your call."

As they were pulling out of the driveway, Brad turned to Jacob and asked, "What was it with Mrs. Barlow that got your attention?"

"I just feel I have seen her somewhere before, or know

someone who looks like her. I can't put my finger on it right now, but it will come to me."

"Knowing you, I'm sure it will. Say, I think we hit pay dirt big time with Katie's Kennel. We need to keep her in mind whenever we need dogs. I have never worked with a golden retriever before, but Lady and I seemed to bond from the first time she looked at me with those very expressive eyes. She seems to be highly intelligent, too."

"So do the three guys. Maybe we should think about talking to the department heads and suggest they contract with Mrs. Mayhew about supplying all our dogs. Not that we will be needing any more new dogs soon, barring any accidents. That is one thing I did NOT tell Mrs. Mayhew. About the danger to the dogs if a drug bust goes ugly, I mean."

"Nope, not something she needs to hear right now."

# Chapter Nine

THE NEXT MORNING, KATIE CAME running into the farmhouse shouting. "Okay, Sam. Let's go car shopping!"

"Can you at least wait until I finished my breakfast?" Sam asked.

"I guess, as long as you don't take too long." Looking around, she added, "Say, where is everybody?"

"Jeff had to go in early to check on a patient, Granny Edi is knitting out on the sunporch, and Meli and Will have gone off on one of their photo jaunts. Meli needs a few more pictures to finish her book, so they drove up to the lake today."

"I hear it is beautiful up there. I need to ask Russell to take me someday. I'll just go out and talk to Granny Edi while you finish up."

Twenty minutes later, they were on their way.

Sam asked, "So where are we going first? Jeff tells me there is a small dealership in the village, but they don't seem to have a very large selection."

"Russell told me to try over in the valley, where there are several dealerships. Let's go there first."

Just after noon, they got back home, and could hardly wait until the after-dinner chat in the family room.

Jeff came in with a cup of coffee in one hand and a slice of Granny's walnut cake in the other. He sat in his favorite chair, sighed contentedly, then asked Sam, "So, my love, how much of my money did you spend on a new car today?"

"Not one cent, you bully! I have been fortunate enough to get enough clients that I could pay for my new car all by myself, thank you very much."

"Well, I like the sound of that! So, what did you get?"

At that, Katie could not hold it in any longer.

"We each now have a car just like Abbi's 'Baby Blu'. We both fell in love with it while she had it here, so decided to get one like it."

Sam added, "Mine is a lovely shade of Sunshine Yellow, and Katie's is green of course."

"Of course it has to be green." Russell said. "I think everything in our house would be green if I didn't put my foot down once in a while."

"Oh, yeah, you are so hard to get along with, Hon. You hardly ever let me have my way."

Granny Edi said, "That is not the way I hear it. From the conversations going around this house, I'd say all of you try very hard to please your spouses. And that pleases me very much. So, are you girls going to name your new purchases like Abbi did with Blu?"

Sam said, "Well, mine sort of named itself. It almost

has to be Buttercup. I'm not sure what Katie can do with green!"

Katie exclaimed, "I'll have you know, I have already figured it out. Isn't there a song that goes something like 'my Lady, Greensleeves? Well, since the sale of Lady gave me enough money to buy it, I thought I might call my little car Greensleeves, but that is just too long. So I tried to think of other things that are green and decided I didn't like 'Peas' either, but I DID like 'Sweet Pea', so that's what I'll call her."

Will spoke up to say, "Whatever their names, you seem to have two cars that will get you around. I have had doubts about Sam's car doing that for some time. Treat them well, Ladies, and they should last as long as her old one did."

Russel said, "Speaking of getting around, I hear you and Meli had an interesting trip today, Will."

"Yeah, and I wanted to talk to you about something we saw up there. And King, too, for that matter. In the small town on the North Shore, there is a beautiful old building. It used to be the one and only hotel, but closed down after a fire pretty much gutted one end several years ago. I don't know if you and King would want to get into the re-construction business, but this could be a great project if you are interested."

"I would have to see it myself, of course, and then check with King. How far is this little town from here?"

"Depending on the route you take, either about

thirty-five or forty miles. Close enough either way that your crews could commute every day."

"And that is a plus. I can't get away this week, but maybe Katie and I can run up that way sometime next week. Might even take this new green machine of my wife's and give it a trial run."

"Oh, yes! I would like that." Katie exclaimed. "Would you like to go with us, Granny Edi?"

"My dear, I'm not sure I could travel that far in your little car. Abbi tried to take me into the village one day in her Blu and I only made it as far as the end of the driveway before I asked to be let out. I may not be able to see the ground but when I sit that low, I can feel it, and it made me uncomfortable."

Will said, "Hey, I have an idea. Let's make it a family day. We can all go up on Saturday. I can drive Granny and Sam in our bigger car, and you guys follow in Sweet Pea. We can make it a day at the beach on the lake, with a picnic at the park, and seeing the country around the lake, then have a nice dinner in the village. That will give Russell time to check out the old hotel, and we can still get back here by bedtime."

Melissa said, "I love that idea. It will give me another chance to take more family pictures."

Will uttered to himself, "How did I know she was going to say that?" Then to the others, "Let's plan to leave early so we have time to check out the roadside fruit stands. They have some of the best peaches around here, and it's getting toward the end of the season. I'd like to get some before they are all gone."

With those plans made, they slowly drifted off to bed.

# Chapter Ten

THE REST OF THE WEEK was quiet, with no word from Jacob Finnigan.

Katie started looking for a suitable mate for her other female golden. This was the first time she did not have a litter of puppies due before the others sold, and she was anxious to remedy that. Lucy was about ready to breed, so Katie was spending time doing the research necessary to assure a good mate for her.

Russell and Will worked on getting the fence up, with help from Jeff when he was not at the hospital. Once the fence was finished, they all began planning for the trip up to the lake. A huge lunch was packed, and they took off early on Saturday morning. Will led them out into the country and took the longer route to the lake. On the way, they found several roadside stands, where Will bought enough peaches that Granny Edi would be busy for the next several days making preserves and pies and even ice cream.

When they finally arrived in the small town of Lakeview on the North Shore, those that had never been there were charmed with the architecture and quaintness. They had a lovely few hours at the beach, and after a very good dinner at one of the two restaurants in town, Will took them all to look at the old hotel. It was several miles outside of town, on a small peninsula jutting into the lake.

Russell liked what he saw, and the ladies fell in love with what was left of it also. Granny Edi said she remembered coming for dances in the ballroom when she was a girl. She also said that some friends her age had told her they would like to come and live in the hotel all the time.

"You mean live here as if it were their home?" Russell asked.

"Well, yes, I guess so. Joyce Simson said she wants to sell her big house just outside our village and find something smaller up here in Lakeview. I guess others would like to retire here, too.

"That's it!" Russell exclaimed.

"What?" Katie asked.

"If King is aggregable to this, instead of just re-building a hotel, we could turn this into a retirement home for senior citizens. With all the new motels and bed and breakfast places I saw on the way here, another hotel is really not needed. With this lake-front view and modern comforts in roomy suites, this would be a great place to retire. Meli, please take a few more pictures so I can send them out to King."

Meli used both her wide-angle and the normal lens to shoot a dozen or so pictures, plus several with her new digital camera, and even a few with her cell phone. She said, "I'll send these few out to him right away, then the more detailed ones later." She dialed King's number and sent the four quick pictures and a very brief message to tell him to expect more the next day.

With that decision made, they headed home. Melissa printed her pictures the next day, and Russell faxed them to King with his ideas for the retirement home. King and Abbi flew in two days later.

Russell and King drove up to the lake, King came back excited about the project, and the two of them disappeared into the Mayhew Construction offices. The rest of the family did not see much of them for several days.

Abbi, Katie, Sam, and Melissa helped Granny Edi finish up the preserving and pie baking, then settled in to spoil the twins and catch up on family news. Katie and Sam took Abbi for rides in their new cars and Melissa took many, many pictures of the twins.

When Jacob Finnigan called, Katie and Sam went out to see the training sessions. When they arrived, Jacob had Lucky in a large area where there were multiple ramps, obstacles, and hiding places. Watching Lucky put through his paces was a rewarding experience for Katie. She knew all her puppies had great potential, but this kind of training was new to her. She had not been sure her dogs were cut out for it, but Lucky seemed to be proving her wrong.

As the team finished the session, Jacob gave a command to Lucky, the dog looked around and saw Katie and Sam. Looking back at Jacob for permission, he then came running up to the women and greeted them warmly.

Jacob walked over to them and told Katie, "I want you to know all three of your puppies have gone above and beyond anything that we expected from dogs this young. They are all partnered now, and living with their new families. And just so you know, Mrs. Mayhew, Lucky is mine! He has fit into my family very quickly and feels it is his duty to protect my three-year-old daughter from all the falls and scrapes a child that age usually gets. I am very happy with him on all levels."

"Why, thank you Mr. Finnigan. I am so glad they are making me proud. And please, call me Katie. And I'm sure my friend would not mind if you call her Sam."

"In that case, my name is Jacob, or Jake to my friends. And I hope we will become friends. My department would like to purchase other dogs from you when we need them. Could you let us know when you have other puppies ready?"

"I would be happy to do that. I have another female that I will be breeding soon, but her pups would probably arrive and be old enough to leave her before you needed them. I think you told me you only needed the three for your teams right now?"

"That's right, but I have contacts in other police departments throughout the country. One of them might need a dog or two. Could you give us the right to get one before you offer them to the general public?"

"Well, sure. I suppose that could be a good thing for both of us."

"You bet! Now, how about a cup of coffee from the snack bar before you head home?"

Katie looked over at Sam and asked, "Do you have time for that?"

"Yes, that would be fine. I don't have to be back until early evening. My new client will be there at six."

"Great! Just let me put Lucky in his kennel here at headquarters, and I will be right with you."

As they settled into a booth in the snack bar, Katie started asking questions about the training process and especially about how her guys were doing.

"As I told you earlier, all three have taken to the training very quickly. We have not worked with goldens before, and the department is a bit surprised at how quickly they learn the new lessons. I have partnered with Connor, my current dog for six years, and he is very good at what he does, but I think Lucky will outshine him once he is fully trained."

Sam asked, "You say you have not worked with goldens before. What other breeds are good at this drug business?"

Jake smiled and said, "Some are better at it than others, of course, but we use mostly German Shepherds. My Connor happens to be a Beagle, and they are as popular as the Shepherds for this line of work."

Katie said, "Thank you so much for letting us watch you and Lucky today. He seems to have fully accepted you as the boss, which I like to see. May I come back sometime near the end of his training so I can see the result of your hard work?"

"I will certainly let you know when would be a good time. And you, too, Sam, if you would like to come. And, if you don't mind my asking, how did you come to be 'Sam'? That does not seem to fit you at all."

Both women laughed, then Sam said, "My full name is Samantha Ann Mathews Barlow, so it was shortened to SAM when I was just a baby."

Katie added, "It's also short for Samson! She is a force to behold when she gets riled."

Jake chuckled, then asked, "If you don't mind me asking, where are you from, Sam?"

Sam looked startled for a moment, then replied, "I was born and raised just outside of Richmond, Virginia. But why do you ask?"

"You remind me of someone, but I just can't place who, or even where I met them. I thought knowing where you were born might jog my memory."

"Ah, I see. However, I'm afraid you are out of luck there. I have no living blood relatives, not even any distant cousins." There was a sad look on her face as she said this, then she smiled and said, "It must be just a 'look-alike' that sometimes happens."

"You are probably right, just a close resemblance, no doubt. At any rate, you are welcome to come with Katie whenever it is convenient."

"Thank you, Jake. It was all very interesting."

As the women drove home, they talked about all they had seen, not only Jake and Lucky, but the other teams going through exercises on the big field. They were very pleased with what they had seen and planned to go often. Katie even considered giving up on her Companion Dog training and going entirely with the Search and Rescue Training program for her own dogs.

# Chapter Eleven

W HEN RUSSELL AND KING FINALLY emerged from their offices, there was a lively discussion in the family room that night. They had contacted the owner of the old hotel and found him more than willing to sell them the property and several additional acres at a very reasonable price.

As King put it, "He told us we were doing him a favor. It seems no hotel owners, or potential owners, are willing to take on the cost of rebuilding. He was getting pretty desperate."

Russell picked up the story. "The town is enthusiastic about our plans and will push through all the permits needed for the conversion from commercial zoning to residential zoning. We still need to apply for all the permits needed to actually start construction, and there is a whole book of state regulations regarding Retirement Homes we will have to read. I have already ordered it, so we should have it soon. Then we can get started as soon as we finish drawing up the plans for what we want to do."

Will asked, "How is this project going to impact the plans for our new barn?"

"Not too much." Russell answered. "Both of my crews

are finishing up the two office buildings they are currently working on. They should be able to put up the barn while we are getting the plans and permits and everything else ready to start at the lake."

Just then, Sam and Abbi came back in. While the guys were talking business, they had gone to the kitchen to get servings of peach cobbler. As they came back carrying the trays, Sam practically shouted. "Guess what Abbi just told me? She got a phone call this afternoon from the Phoenix Fabrics manager. He is ready to start our first run early next month! We are in business!"

Granny Edi said, "Well, it sounds like we have a lot to celebrate tonight! Russell, will you get that bottle of plum wine from the shelf in the kitchen? Meli, please take my knitting and put it in the drawer so Cisco can't get it. He still hides it whenever he can find it lying around."

Abbi spoke up to say, "Is that monkey still causing problems with his hide and seek games? I thought he would have given up by now."

"Nope!" Will said. "You would never know it to look at him now though. All 'Mr. Innocence' wrapped around Charlie and blissfully sleeping on the window seat. Why that cat puts up with him I can't figure out."

Meli said, "It's because they practically grew up together. Those two have been buddies for a long time."

Abbi turned to Sam and asked, "Speaking of Charlie, would you let me have two of the kittens he fathered? Two of the ones that look the most like him? I would like the twins to each have a pet and this idea seems like the best choice right now."

"Well, I guess the twins ARE a bit young for King to put them on the back of a horse! Sure, take any two you like, but ask Meli too. Her grandmother gave Charlie to both of us you know, so the kittens are half hers."

Meli chimed in with, "Take as many as you like! The more you take will mean fewer we have to find homes for. Ten barn cats are about six too many!"

"And speaking of buddies," Sam said, "Prince, I know you are Granny Edi's buddy, but you are going to have to move over so she can eat her cobbler. Katie, what is it with your goldens? They all think they should be lap dogs! Even if their rumps are firmly on the floor, they still seem to manage to get most of the rest of them into somebody's lap if they are even slightly encouraged."

Granny asked, "Are you saying I encourage Prince to misbehave?"

"Well, now that you mentioned it, you have spoiled him a bit. He is definitely not the well behaved Companion Dog Katie trained him to be."

Granny reached for her dish of cobbler, then said, "He is retired! Don't you remember Katie telling us that? If he is retired, he deserves to have the rules overlooked sometimes. We old ones need special consideration, don't we, Prince?"

Prince woofed as if he knew exactly what she had said,

then dropped down to the floor and put his head on her feet.

Katie said, "You talking about the Companion Dog training, I think I see some changes coming up in that area. After visiting with Jake Finnigan and seeing what he is doing with Lucky, I am leaning toward doing that with any more puppies that I have. Lucy will be ready to breed in a couple of weeks, and I think I will ask Jake how to get started."

Russell asked, "Don't you want to consider still training a few as Companion Dogs, love? I know you had a great sense of satisfaction when you could place one of them with a physically challenged individual, especially children."

"You are right, that was a good feeling. Maybe I can do both. There might be some sort of test to see which puppies would best fit in which program. I guess I need to talk with Jake Finnigan again. So, to change the subject, what are your initial plans for the Retirement Home?"

"First, I would like to hire more workers so we can get the job done before winter." Russell said. "I understand a bad one is expected and I'd like to at least have the exterior completed before the first snow."

King replied, "About that very subject. While we were flying East, Abbi had a good idea, Russell. I had told her that if we really want to get this project well under way before winter, we are going to need more workers. She suggested you might want to get in touch with your old friend, Simon Nobles. Do you think he might be interested in working with us?"

"Hey, that's a great idea! I haven't heard from Si in a long time, so I don't know what his commitments are, but I'll give him a call. It would be great working with him again."

Cobbler eaten and people beginning to yawn, the family soon broke up and went to bed.

# Chapter Twelve

RUSSELL CAME INTO THEIR KITCHEN the next morning to find Katie standing at the window, coffee cup in hand.

"Penny for them, Hun. You seem deep in thought. What is going through that wonderful mind of yours?"

"Oh, just looking at that beautiful green mountain of ours. I am still getting used to the idea of us actually owning it. There's more coffee, but I haven't started breakfast yet. I'm waiting for Abbi and King to come over so we can decide what we want."

"Super. I'll get a cup of coffee, then head to the home office and call Si. I'd like to catch him before he starts his day."

"Fine. I'll call you when we are ready to eat."

Just as Katie finished her coffee, Abbi and King entered the room, each carrying a child.

"Oh, let me hold one of them. You can put the other one in a highchair, and we can start breakfast."

King spoke up, "Here, take Rona, please! She is very cranky this morning, so I'll be happy to cook while you deal with her!"

Abbi added, "I think both of them are beginning to

get a couple of teeth, but Ren seems to be handling it better than his sister. What's on the menu this morning?"

"Almost anything you like. Fresh eggs, of course, and I bought some bagels yesterday. Or pancakes? Whatever." She sat down with Rona in her lap and started playing with her.

King turned from the refrigerator with eggs in his hand. "How about one of my famous omelets? And, I must say, I really think Russell's idea to have a shared kitchen and living room for both sides of this floor was brilliant! We are not here often enough to need a separate space in our apartment, and it's nice to share when we do come. Where is he, by the way?"

"In his office up here, calling Si. He probably wanted an answer before you guys went to the business offices. We are to call him when his breakfast is ready."

"Or not!" Abbi said. "Here he is already."

"Good morning." Russell said as he came into the kitchen. He put out a hand to ruffle the hair on Ren's head as he passed by the highchair and was rewarded with a big smile from the baby. Then Russell continued, "Abbi, that was a wonderful idea you had. Si was very receptive to the whole plan for the Retirement Home, but has a couple of houses to finish up before he can join us."

"That's great!" Katie said. "I will like getting to know him better. Too bad Jenny and Joel can't come with him."

King spoke up. "Hey, why can't they? Russell, let's run up to the site today and see what is left on the side of the hotel that did not burn. There may be enough left that we could clean it up for Si's family to move into. They would not have any of the amenities of a functioning hotel of course, but there may be beds available and maybe a chair or two. Jenny and their son can 'camp out' at the lake for a few weeks. Didn't you tell me she is homeschooling him, so he will not miss any classes. Since it is still Summer, that wouldn't be a problem anyway. I expect Si will be here for much longer than that, but it could be a nice vacation for them. What about Si's crew, Russell?"

"He is checking into that and asked if we knew of a campground close to the site. We can check on that while we are up there today. He said that most of his crew already have travel trailers they could bring, and possibly share with the ones that don't. He will tell them about the project today, and see how many would be willing to bring up their campers."

"Sounds like a plan. Let's finish up here so we can get on the road! We will leave the dishes for you girls, right?"

"Of course." Katie said. "What else will we do with ourselves today, Abbi?"

"Do you think Sam or Meli would watch the babies for a couple of hours? I would dearly love to ride up to the top of your Green Mountain."

"Let's ask! That sounds like fun and I haven't been on a horse in weeks."

Dishes done and beds made, Katie and Abbi took the

twins through the connecting door into the family room of the farmhouse. They found Sam and Granny out on the sun porch enjoying cups of coffee and a chat about what needed to be done with the flower beds to prepare them for winter. Melissa and Will were both in their shared office, busy working on their latest books.

When asked about the babysitting, Granny jumped at the chance.

"Let's take them into the family room and settle them into their playpens with their toys. Since Meli will be right across the hall, I can call her if needed. That way, Sam can go with you if she wants to."

"Oh, yes! I would like that."

# Chapter Thirteen

O UT IN THE BARN, THE ladies stopped to pick up bridles, then went out into the pasture to collect the horses. Abbi came back with Star, Katie had her Thunder, and Sam had Eclipse.

As she started to saddle up, Sam said, "I hate to leave poor Spider by himself. He looked so lonely when we brought the others in. Too bad Will is tied up in his book. He could have come with us."

"Hey, thanks for thinking of me, Sis." Will said as he walked into the barn. "As of about ten minutes ago, the book is all finished, and when Granny told me where you ladies were going, I thought I would tag along. Looks like I won't even have to chase down Spider to get a bridle on him. He must have followed you and is standing right by the gate."

They all finished with the saddling, went to the back of the pasture and started up the trail. When they reached the top of the mountain, they dismounted to rest for a few minutes.

"Tell me more about what I am seeing, Will." Katie said. "I would like to know about my neighbors on the other two sides."

"Well, to begin with, just down there at the foot of your green mountain is the boundary of Webber's Organic Vegetable Farm. He actually owns several hundred acres, going all the way beyond the base of Sam and Jeff's place on that side but most of it stretching out on the other to the back and side of your property. His family has had a farm there for several generations, but he just turned it into an organic operation about ten years ago. I understand from the gossip in our village that he supplies most of the fancy restaurants and hotels in the valley with produce. He also has a small outlet shop right there at his farm."

Sam said, "And why are we just now finding out about this place? I would have loved to know where to shop for fresh produce long before now!"

"Oops!" Will said. "I guess it just never occurred to me that you weren't happy with the grocery store here in the village."

"There is nothing wrong with the store, and they usually have everything I want, but shopping at a Farmer's Market is great fun. Katie, Abbi, let's go over and see if he has any pumpkins for Halloween decorations."

"Oooooh! I haven't carved a pumpkin since I was a kid!" Abbi said. "That would be great!"

As she looked out over the valley below, Katie said, "I was just telling Russell this morning how much I love my green mountain. It was so wonderful of your grandmother to give us this place, Will."

Sam added, "Yes, indeed. There just not enough words

to describe how much Jeff and I appreciate our portion of Melrose Farm. You and Granny Edi have been very generous, Will."

"And let me add my thanks, also." Abbi chimed in. "That trust fund was a wonderful surprise."

"Whoa! You are embarrassing me." Will said. "Stop with all the thanks already. I should be thanking you! As I told you earlier, I no longer have to worry about what to do with the place, and that is a burden off my shoulders. Now, let's start down so we can get lunch. I'm starving."

By the time they had gotten back to the barn, unsaddled and brushed down the horses, and gotten themselves into the house, Meli and Granny Edi had lunch ready. Between bites of their lunch, all except Will happily made plans to visit the organic farm soon. Granny said that it might be a good time to stock up on things she could 'put by' for the winter ahead.

When the three young women asked her what she meant, she laughed at them, then explained.

"People of my generation would 'put by' or can as much of their summer harvest of vegetables and fruits as they could so they would have them to eat during the winter months. We made cucumber pickles, watermelon pickles, pickled peaches, canned green beans, corn, lima beans, tomatoes, whatever we grew in the garden over the spring and summer. That is also why there are so many old fruit trees in my back yard. My parents loved to have a good supply of fruit preserves 'put by' for the winter. Nothing like opening a new jar of fig or peach preserves or apple butter for your hot biscuits on Christmas morning!"

All Will said was, "I'll buy it if you ladies will handle the rest. I'll even put up more shelves in the basement to hold it all."

# Chapter Fourteen

AFTER LUNCH, THEY ALL SEPARATED to do their own thing, mostly taking naps.

That evening the after-dinner chat centered mostly around what Russell and King had found out up at the lake. They reported the hotel had several rooms that could be easily cleaned and made comfortable for not only Si and his family, but most of Si's construction crew as well. Although there was a small campground nearby, King and Russell saw no need to add the expense of renting spaces there for the crew. By collecting beds and dressers from unused areas, there would be plenty of bedrooms for all the workers.

They had also climbed into the burned section to access what needed to be done there. The rubble had never been cleared away, so there was going to be a major job just getting the site cleared.

Sam asked, "Hey, guys, what is the condition of the furniture? I mean, most of it is pretty old I would guess. Can some of it be salvaged and sold? A lot of people might like to buy antiques just to say they came from that old hotel."

"Excellent idea, Sam!" Abbi said. "My other home

was filled with antiques 'The Jerk' had collected. When I had it auctioned off before I sold the house, those things brought in a lot of money. That might help pay for some of the restorations, King!"

"Sounds like something we need to check out." King said. "Can we turn the job of locating what can be saved and organizing the sale to you ladies? However, do not even think about going into the burned out section yourselves. After what we saw today, I don't want you ladies near that danger. We can have our crews locate any furniture that survived the fire and bring it to you. They are used to climbing around with just beams for support, so are less likely to get hurt."

Abbi said, "Works for me. Can they put it in the old ballroom for now? That would give us space to clean it up and see what can be saved. How much damage to the furniture do you think there will be?"

Russell said, "The fire started on the third floor, and the floors below suffered only water damage. However, the building has been neglected so long, we think there may be a lot of mold growing in the walls, and the wood floors are badly rotted in places. We think we will probably be better off just taking it all down and starting over. But, that also means any upholstered furniture will probably be moldy. We may want to stick with just the wood and metal pieces that can be cleaned easily."

"Taking it all down will mean a longer time before we can actually start the conversion from a hotel to a retirement home." King said, "but it will also mean we can build the new section as retirement apartments from the beginning. That way, we can make them a little larger than we would have had by converting two hotel rooms into one apartment."

Russell said, "The other end, the one that did not burn, has some smoke damage, but that can easily be fixed with a good scrubbing and new paint. The lobby area, ballroom, some meeting rooms, and the basement kitchen all just need a good clean-up and fresh paint. As we convert to the new apartments on the upper five floors, we will be tearing out some dividing walls, so will not even have to consider repainting them."

King spoke up, "All in all, I think this is going to be a very interesting and potentially very profitable venture. Will and Jeff, on the drive back today, Russell and I talked about asking if either of you might want to become business partners in this. We could turn it into a family owned business and take advantage of the tax breaks that would mean."

Jeff looked at Sam, and she nodded. He said, "I think we could come up with some capital to do this. Just don't ask us to start swinging hammers. What about you Will?"

"Sounds interesting, but I have been thinking about another investment we should look into. On the ride I took with the girls this morning, it occurred to me that if you guys and Meli had been there, we could not have ridden out together. I was thinking that since we are planning a new barn, we should plan to make it big enough so that we can each have a horse. I know we don't always need eight horses, but it would be nice to have them when Abbi and King are here. I just don't know where to go to buy them without breaking the bank. I know horses aren't cheap!"

Abbi said, "I think I know of a way we can get all the horses we could ever want, and still leave you enough money to invest in the retirement home venture if you want to!

"Jeff, remember the wonderful horse rescue farm where I stopped at the beginning of my 'running away' trip? I bet if we talked to Mr. O'Shay he might have a horse or two that are well enough to go to another home. That would only mean a donation to his farm if you wish."

"All right!" Will exclaimed. "Then count me in on the other 'family venture'. Abbi, could you call your Mr. O'Shay tomorrow? We will not have to get the horses until the new barn is finished, but it won't hurt to ask now so he can be on the lookout for us."

Sam very quietly asked, "Do you think he might find a small pony for me?"

Everyone laughed at that. Sam was rather short and was not a very good horsewoman, so they all knew her concern. As she had said before, a small horse would put her closer to the ground when she fell off.

King spoke up. "Don't worry about two horses for Abbi and me. We can just bring two from Castle Ranch.

No need to buy horses when our brother has an entire herd running around."

"But won't Bob object to you taking away some of his horses?" Sam asked.

"Since Katie sold her share of the ranch back to us, I own a full 50 percent of it." King said. "Bob can't object to me bringing two of my own horses here! We will just have to make plans to drive Abbi's camper/trailer the next time we come. We could bring one for you too, Sam, but all of Bob's stock are full quarter-horses, so they would be taller than you like."

Sam said, "Oh, that's okay King. I can just wait and see what Mr. O'Shay can find. Will you call him before you leave, Abbi?"

"Sure thing, bright and early tomorrow. And speaking of tomorrow morning, it's time to get my two munchkins in bed. Thank you for rocking Rona, Granny Edi. King, can you please bring Ren?"

Since Abbi and King were planning to fly back to Texas the next day, they did not stay to talk longer. King had a few jobs to finish up, and Abbi needed to complete three costumes so she could ship them out. They were to be back soon so King could help get the hotel renovations project started. As they left, everyone else called it a night and went to bed.

# Chapter Fifteen

RUSSELL CALLED SI THE NEXT morning to talk about the project and was happy to hear that every one of Si's crew was looking forward to the new project. Even the fact that the lake was several hundred miles from their home did not seem to bother them. Most were bachelors, and the rest planned to bring their wives for some of the time they would be working at the lake.

It would be good to work with Si again. They had started a construction company together many years ago, but due to events in their lives, they had drifted apart and settled in different parts of the country.

As Russell walked back into the kitchen, King asked him, "Everything good to go with Si?"

"Yes, he can come up in about two weeks with several of his crew. He said Jenny was also looking forward to a break from her usual routine. In the meantime, we can get started on the cleaning up of the rooms for him and Jenny and get my crew doing the demolition work on the other end. Maybe we can have that done by the time Si gets here so we can begin the actual construction. I think we can hire someone from the town up there to do the cleaning. I seem to remember seeing a commercial cleaning business when we went up the first time."

"Yes, and we also need to finish up the drawings for how we plan to turn the existing rooms into retirement apartments. The rebuilding of the burned section will not be as difficult. We know we have to start from scratch there, so we can pretty much build it out just like we would several small houses all put together. They will be the three and four bedroom units, correct?"

"Yep. Say, Katie came up with a suggestion late last night that I want to run by you. She suggested we name the project 'Bradley Place' to honor Granny Edi and thank her for her very generous gifts, and especially since she is really the one that gave me the idea of turning the hotel into a retirement home."

"I think that is a wonderful idea! I had been wondering how we were going to get away from 'The Lakefront Hotel' name. Let's go over and ask her how she feels about that right after we have breakfast."

Katie and Abbi were just putting the meal on the table, so it wasn't long before all of them headed down in the home elevator and through the connecting door into the family room.

Everyone was there except Jeff, who had already left for early rounds at the hospital.

Russell approached Granny Edi where she was sitting in her favorite easy chair with her knitting in her lap. He knelt in front of her and took one of her hands into both of his.

"Mrs. Edith Melrose Bradley, if I can please interrupt your knitting for just a few minutes, I have a very important question to ask you."

"My, my! Aren't we formal this morning? You know you can interrupt me at any time. What is it?"

"Well, it's about this project of turning the old hotel up at the lake into a retirement home. Since it was your comment about your friends wanting to live up there that gave me the idea, King and I would like to name it 'Bradley Place' in your honor."

"Oh, Russell, you and King don't have to do that!"

"But we want to, Granny Edi. You could say it's our way of saying another 'Thank You' for all you have done for us. And it was actually Katie who came up with the idea. She wants to thank you, too!"

Abbi said, "I think that is a wonderful gesture. We all owe you big time for being so generous. This will be a small part of how much you're appreciated by your 'grandchildren'."

As one, Sam, Will, and Meli shouted their agreement, and Granny searched in her pocket for a large handkerchief.

Then Will asked when they would be going back up to the lake to look around.

King said, "Sometime later this morning. I am waiting on a couple of calls from people getting the paperwork finished, then we will go up. I haven't given them my cell phone number yet, so have to rely on the house phone for right now. I'll take care of that little detail when they call. While we are up at the lake we need to hire a little local help to clear away the rubble while the weather still holds. Then Abbi and I really should to get back to Texas."

Granny said, "You boys be careful crawling around in that mess. I'm sure a lot of it is not safe, particularly the top floors. Don't take any chances and end up falling through several stories!"

Russell assured her they would be careful, then he and King went back to the Mayhew Construction offices to work on plans for the new apartments while they waited for the phone calls.

That evening, Doc Simmons came over to join them for the nightly chat. Since he had given up his position as Chief of Staff for the hospital and turned everything over to Jeff, he visited several times a week. He said he looked forward to the visits as a way to chase away some of the boredom of having no job to go to. As Jeff caught him up on what was going on at the hospital, a wistful expression came over his face. Sam saw it, and rightly guessed that he was lonely, and needed something to do with his life.

# Chapter Sixteen

A S HAPPENS SOMETIMES IN A group, there was a break in the conversation while everyone took a bite of their dessert at the same time. Sam took a deep breath, then asked as casually as possible,

"Russell? This new project of yours will be a retirement home, right? There will be elderly folks living there, some on several medications, and others physically challenged in some way, correct? What, if any, plans do you have to provide medical care for them? Will they have to go into the town if they need to see a doctor?"

"Ouch! You do know how to ask embarrassing questions, don't you, Sis?" Russell said. "Unfortunately, I had not even considered that issue and King hasn't said anything about it either. And you are right, a place housing retirees should have some kind of medical care available on site."

"I guess being married to a doctor makes me a little more aware of the problem than most." Sam said as she smiled at Jeff. "But now that I have presented you with a problem, may I also offer a solution? Why don't you ask Doc Simmons if he could help in setting up a clinic there? If he could start an entire hospital here in our village, surely it should not be too difficult to do a small clinic. Right, Doc?"

"What are you talking about, girl? I haven't been over here every day and seem to have missed out on something! What is this about a retirement home, and why am I the last to know?"

They all chuckled, then Russell told him about the new project he and King were starting.

He then added, "I think Sam has a great idea, Doc, if you are willing to take on the challenge. We are just at the beginning of the design phase, so adding space for a clinic will be easy to do. If you will help with this, you can us tell us what is needed, like how much room should we commit to the clinic area."

"Give me some time to think about this." Doc Simmons said as he took another bite of cake. He chewed, swallowed, then said, "Okay, enough thinking. I would be happy to be a part of this project. This area is long overdue for a place like you are proposing and the lake area is a beautiful location for it. I remember that old hotel fondly and the dances Clarissa and I would go to in the summer. Remember them, Edith? I believe you were dating Ralph Gilroy at the time." At her nod, he continued, "It will be nice seeing something done with it, other than just letting it fall down. When can we start the designing part?"

Russell said, "Why don't you come with us tomorrow? King and I went early this morning, and feel really optimistic about what needs to be done. It would help to get your opinion early on as to where your clinic should go."

They arrived in Lakeside about mid-morning the next day. Stopping at a small cafe, they ordered coffee and asked their waitress about hiring local help. She told them about the commercial cleaning company and gave them directions to a small office just outside of town. They were able to hire enough workers to scrub and then paint the unburned part of the hotel, starting in three days. They would begin with several rooms for Si and his family, then the ballroom where Russell and King wanted to set up their on-site office, then the rest of the rooms, expecting to complete all of it in two-to-three weeks.

Russell then drove them out to the old hotel. As they walked around the grounds, Doc Simmons was delighted to see it again, even in the dilapidated state.

"You say you were able to purchase several additional acres?"

Russell answered, "Yes, about seven actually. We have talked about eventually putting in a small putting green, a tennis court, and an outdoor swimming pool, and maybe even a small area where the residents can do some gardening if they wish."

"What would you think of the idea of separating the clinic from the main building by a short walkway? And maybe even adding a small addition on the side as living quarters for a doctor-in-residence?"

Russell questioned, "What are you thinking, Doc? It sounds to me as if you are asking a personal question!"

"You have gotten to know me well, Russell. Yes, it was a bit personal. That house I live in now was wonderful when I still had Clarissa, but it is now way too big and lonely for me. I've been thinking about selling it for years, but just never could decide where I would go if I did sell. Now you boys have given me the perfect answer! If you would let me be the resident doctor here, I could run the clinic, and have lots of old folks like me around for card games or checkers or just to talk to. I could still visit at Edith's once or twice in a month, but I hate to butt in there all the time."

"Well, as far as I'm concerned, you've made yourself a deal, although I am quite sure no one at Melrose Farm thinks you butt in. We love to have you come to visit. But I can see where you could get lonely and bored living alone. This could possibly be a good fit for you. Shall we start the renovations by building your clinic and new home first? Having a doctor and working clinic already available would be a good selling point for potential residents, not to mention any injuries to our carpenters, so it would work in our favor too. Would that be too soon for you, Doc?"

"Not at all. It will take some time to contact sources for clinic equipment and to sell my house. I should be able to move up here almost as soon as you get the clinic built."

"Great!" King said. "Let's walk around the property

once more and decide on the location. Not too far from the main building but far enough away to give you some privacy, right?"

"Yes, and I think I know just the place. I seem to remember a small cove over on the far side of the unburned section. Seems to me that would be a nice spot, especially if you ever want to expand the clinic to have a small infirmary. That would be a pretty place to have a few beds if anyone needs to recuperate for a few days."

When they got to the spot Doc had recommended, they both agreed it would be perfect. Only about one hundred yards from the side entrance of the old hotel, on flat ground making it easy walking for the elderly, it was separated from the building by a small flower garden, bushes, and a few large trees.

Russell exclaimed, "This would be perfect! The kitchen is on this side, too, so any deliveries or emergency vehicles could come up the driveway right over there. So, Doc, if you needed an ambulance for a patient they could come almost to the door of the clinic."

"This is going to be wonderful!" Doc said. "Now let's get back home so we can start drawing up the plans for my space. I also need to contact a Real Estate person to get my house listed and look into ordering supplies."

As they walked back to the car, Russell said. "We can start on tearing down the burned section right away, but as soon as the painting is finished in the other part, we can start building out and filling those apartments with new residents. That way, we will have more working capital to re-build the burned out part."

The guys, including Doc Simmons, were very animated at the after-dinner chat that evening.

Granny Edi was shocked that her brother-in-law had even been thinking about selling his home. "My sister loved that house, and now you want to sell it and move away?"

"Oh, Edith, Clarissa has been gone a long time now, and I found since I retired that the house is too quiet with just me. I didn't notice it so much while I still worked at the hospital all the time, but sometimes now I feel like I am the only person in the world. You know how far from the village I am. I need to be more a part of things, even if it is only old folks with walkers, wheelchairs, and canes. And I'm sure there will be residents at Bradley Place that still have their wits about them and will make nice friends for me. Please don't be upset with me for searching for some companionship in my declining years."

"Clifford, you shame me." Granny Edi said. "Of course you are lonely and now that I think about it, you are right to do this. However, you must come back to see us at least once a week!"

"That is a promise I think I can keep, but let's just see how busy I get. What with all the Bingo, and Checkers, and Chess, and Bridge, and a good gossip session with my new cronies, I may not make it every week!"

# Chapter Seventeen

THINGS WENT ALONG VERY QUICKLY in the next few weeks. The rooms Si would move into were cleaned and painted, the ballroom was being turned into the Melrose Family Enterprises, Inc. offices, and one of Russell's crews had started the construction on the clinic. They had used the other crew to rip out some walls and turn what had been two or even three hotel rooms into small apartments, and the central kitchen was being cleaned, painted, and upgraded. They intended to hire a cook right away and use the facility to feed the crews.

Then disaster struck, in the form of governmental paperwork.

Russell was at the site one day when an official car pulled into the courtyard in front of the hotel. He was served with a summons to appear in court to answer charges of stealing the hotel and property from the rightful owner. The sale was being contested by the great-grandson of the couple who had sold the property to the hotel. He was claiming he had just discovered a will the couple had written leaving the property to his grandfather, then they sold the farm to the hotel. He was saying that the man Russell and King purchased the property from had no rights to it, and he was suing both parties for damages.

Immediately phoning both King and Jessie Davis, Russell called a halt on the clinic construction, dismissed all the workers, and drove home. Once there, he gathered all the files dealing with his purchase, then drove into the village to meet with Jessie. She started an investigation into the paperwork having to do with his purchase of the burned-out property, and then went to the county courthouse to do her own title search, through several more changes of ownership before that. This took time, of course, and put the retirement home project very much behind schedule.

A court date was finally set, King flew in to testify, and King, Russell, and Jessie felt they were ready to present a good argument. When the other side presented their case, it was based entirely on some hand written papers the great grandson had recently found in his grandfather's attic. Jessie was able to prove from the records she had searched, that the original owners had a title to the property in the form of an entry in the court records of the time. They had sold it legally to the hotel, also covered by entries in the county records. She stated that there was no record of any will whatsoever, only a notation that stated all personal property was to be given to their son, who was not even the grandfather of the man who had brought the suit against them. At that, the other side withdrew their complaint, and the case was dismissed.

She told King and Russell later that in her investigation, she had found several people with the same names, to the point that it was sometimes hard to figure out just who was being talked about. She felt the whole case was because of mistaken identities of ancestors.

King went back to Texas happy about the court case, but upset about the delays it had caused. He decided to cut his time in his Texas office short and get back to help Russell however he could. He may not be able to swing a hammer, but he could surely help supervise the crew!

By that time, the weather had turned cold and they knew winter was well on the way.

As soon as the clinic and Doc's lodgings were completed, and all the small apartments finished, they would be ready to continue on the demolition of the burned-out section. By that time, Si and his crew should be there, and they would have three crews working on the project.

Russell, King, and Doc were there almost every day to check on the progress. Along with the temporary re-do of the ballroom into office space, Russell and King had saved a corner for storage to collect the furniture the girls were going to sell, and a portion to serve as a temporary living room area and dining space. They had been able to salvage a couple of sofas, a few tables, a few mismatched chairs, a working drink vending machine, and even a small T.V. from other parts of the hotel, which gave them a comfortable place to relax. Russell had added an extra coffee machine from his home office, and one day this is where they headed for a rest and cup of coffee before going back home. They had just settled in with their coffee when someone walked in the door.

"Si! What are you doing here so early?" Russell exclaimed as he jumped up to greet his friend. "I thought you couldn't get away for another few days."

"My crew can't come until they finish the house they are working on. It was only started to give them something to do while you were having fun in court. However, as boss, I took the opportunity to escape early. I left my foreman in charge and came on up. I couldn't wait any longer to see this new project you have taken on. I called your house this morning, only to find that you were already on your way here, and Katie told me to come on up, so here I am."

"Well, I'm glad you seem so anxious to get started! This is Doctor Clifford Simmons, who will run the clinic here at the retirement home. Doc Simmons is also a friend of the family. And this is King Cole, the other half of Mayhew-Cole Construction. Si Nobles, guys." After handshakes all around, Russell indicated a chair for Si, and went to the coffee machine. "Still take it black? How long can you stay, Si?"

"Just overnight. I plan to get a motel room here in Lakeside for tonight and start back tomorrow morning. I have to get back to oversee the final build-out of that house, but I wanted to see what I had signed up for! I looked around the outside before coming in here, and I like what I see so far. How soon can I bring up my family and crew?"

"Well, as you probably noticed, there isn't much here just yet, however, your quarters are about ready. We still have to cut a door between your living room and one of the hotel rooms to make a bedroom for Joel, but the rest is pretty much finished. You and Jenny have a bedroom on the other end, and all three rooms have a marvelous view of the lake. We even added a tiny kitchen in one corner of the living room. That way, when you and your family go back home, we can use that apartment for the retirement home. I'd say another three days, and the rooms are yours anytime you come back. The crew is a different matter. We need to get a few more bedrooms cleaned and painted before they can be used. Maybe a week?"

"Great! I can't tell you how much I'm looking forward to working with you again. But don't waste your time preparing rooms for my crew. Their wives have outvoted us! They are looking forward to all living in the campground, and calling it their vacation at "Summer Camp". A few of the unmarried workers will stay here, but the others will not need rooms."

Russell added, "It will be good to argue over how long a board should be cut or what size nail is best for the job, just like we used to! Remember those days when we were just getting into the trade? We have both learned a lot since then, but I'm sure we will still argue some! Say, no need to get a room somewhere else. Katie and I have an extra room. Leave your car parked here and stay with us tonight, then come back here tomorrow with King and me."

"If you are sure Katie wouldn't mind, I'd love to do that. It will give me a chance to see what you and King did with that old barn, and maybe even get to meet this Granny Edi you talk so much about."

Russell said, "Then let's head home and continue this discussion there. I'm sure the rest of the family will like to get in on it!"

"Yes, especially Edith." Doc said. "She wouldn't like to be left out!"

Russell explained, "Doc is Granny Edi's brother-in-law, so has known her longer than any of us except Will. And Doc is right, she doesn't like to be left out of our conversations."

# Chapter Eighteen

RUSSELL USED HIS CELL PHONE to call Katie as they were leaving, so she and Abbi had dinner ready when the guys got there. While Abbi and Katie cleaned up after they ate, King and Russell gave Si a tour of their downstairs offices, a peek into Katie's Kennels, and then got him settled into the guest room. Then they all joined the rest of the family for the usual chat before bedtime.

Russell said, "Us construction guys need to get back to the lake early in the morning to finalize the next steps for the retirement home. Doc, do you want to come with us?"

"Not this time, thank you. I need to order a few medical supplies for the clinic. I didn't realize I would need them so soon, but it just occurred to me, there will be cuts and scrapes with all of the crews, and there is no need to come all the way back to the village for a bandage. Will it be all right if I set up a temporary first-aid station in the ballroom?"

"Of course you can." King said. "And you are right, injuries are bound to occur, hopefully only minor ones. The clinic and your apartment should be completed soon, but use any space you need until then. And hearing this made me think that we really need to get the land-line phone service connected as soon as possible. I know most people use their cell phones these days, but it would be nice to have both options."

"Exactly!" Doc said, "And with the three crews working and Si living there, we should probably get the kitchen staff on board soon also. That would keep them from having to go into town to eat and would save time at the lunch hour, plus making the evening meal easier on Jenny."

Russell asked, Doc, "Do you think you will use the central kitchen for your meals, or use your own kitchen? Not that it matters, I'm just curious."

"Oh, most likely, a little of both. Probably my own at first, but as I get to know the residents, I might like to eat with them occasionally. It might depend on the quality of the meals your new chef puts out!"

"I'm glad you said that, Clifford." Granny Edi said. "I have been waiting for a break in the conversation to tell you some good news. Rosie called me from the diner today. She had just heard of the retirement home project and wants to talk to Russell or King before they hire a cook. As you know, she plans to retire herself soon and will leave Rosie's Place to her niece, who has just six months of school before she will come home to start taking over. Rosie suggested you might want to consider the cook she has now. She said Betsy is very good, but there is no future for her at the diner, as Jane will be the head chef when she gets back."

"I love Betsy's cooking!" Doc exclaimed. "If you hire her, I'm thinking my own kitchen will get very little use!"

Will spoke up. "But what will Aunt Rosie do for a cook if you hire Betsy now? You said cousin Jane has to finish cooking school."

"Rosie said she can handle it for that long with some help from the rest of her staff. She used to do it all herself, you know. She just sees this as a good opportunity for Betsy to have her own kitchen to supervise."

Russell said, "I'll call tomorrow and set up an interview."

Katie added, "Wow! This project has taken on a life of it's own! It seems to be going forward so quickly."

Sam said, "Yes, it seems that everything is falling into place remarkably well. We are on our way to another adventure!"

Meli said, "Didn't you warn us of just that a few weeks ago?"

# Chapter Nineteen

"WELL, SINCE YOU WILL BE up here so soon, Si, I guess there is no reason for me to stick around. I would probably just be in the way at this stage anyway." King said. "I'll leave tomorrow, get some work done there in Texas, then plan to come back with my family soon."

Abbi, King, and the twins flew in late in the evening four days later, which barely gave them time to grab a quick dinner and get the twins settled in bed. Knowing the next day was going to be busy, they all retired early.

By the time Katie woke up the next morning, her husband was nowhere to be found. Abbi walked into the kitchen juggling her two babies just as the coffee finished, and said. "Did you get a note, too? Our husbands just had to get back to the site early."

Katie answered, "Yes, they seem very involved with this thing. Oh, well. The sooner it is finished, the sooner we can get the new barn finished and then I can expand my kennel. Russell told me as long as I leave room for my car and his truck, I can put as many dogs in there as I like."

"How many more do you want? You already have six!"

"Yes, but three of them will be sold as I finish their

training. That will leave only Rusty and the two females. I would like to get at least one more male and possibly another female. That would assure me of at least one litter ready for training almost all the time. It is really the only way I can make Katie's Kennel a profitable venture."

"With Russell's successful construction business, I'm not certain you need to worry about adding to the family finances!"

"Maybe not, but you know how independent I am. I like to make my own money, and not depend on Russell for every dime."

"True! You and I are alike in that respect. Now, I'll get these dishes taken care of while you finish getting dressed. What are our plans for the rest of the day?"

"I want to check with the other ladies and see if there is anything I can do to help out. Sam said something yesterday about doing a grocery run over to that big store in the valley. Maybe we could tag along."

When she came back into the kitchen about ten minutes later she said to Abbi, "Looks like my plans for the day have changed. While I was dressing, I got a call from Jake. He would like to see me about one of the dogs he bought. I don't know what the problem is, but maybe it is something I can easily retrain out of whichever dog is having difficulties."

"Oh, well in that case, I think I'll take some sewing and plan to spend the day with Granny Edi. I also need to get in touch with Mr. O'Shay again and see if he has found a horse for Sam."

"Okay. Go get your sewing while I finish giving Ren the last of his cereal."

When Abbi came back into the kitchen, she found Katie in tears.

"I'm ready. I... Oh, Katie, what's wrong?"

"It's nothing. I...oh, I just get so sad sometimes when I look at these two wonderful babies. Don't get me wrong! I love them to pieces, and I'm so glad you have them, but it sometimes makes me sad to be around them."

"Why?" Abbi questioned. "What is it about my babies that makes you sad?"

"Abbi, you mean you can't guess? I thought my brother would have told you by now."

"Told me what, Katie? You know King doesn't share other peoples' secrets."

Katie nodded, took a deep sigh, wiped the remaining cereal from Ren's chin, then turned to Abbi and said, "It's no secret, really. I just don't talk about it. I get sad when I look at your children because it reminds me that I can never have any of my own."

"What!"

"Let's put these angels into their playpen, get another cup of coffee, and I'll tell you the whole story."

When they were again seated at the kitchen table, Katie drank about half of her coffee, gathering her thoughts before she began.

"When the three of us were growing up on the ranch, I followed my brothers everywhere. Well almost everywhere. There were a few of their escapades they refused to let me join. However, there came a day when I made up my mind that I absolutely would not be left behind.

"Both Bob and King said I could not go with them, but I waited until they left and then followed them at a distance. I was about eight or nine at the time, and just knew I could do anything they could do. And that included catching and riding a wild stallion they had seen up on one of the high ranges. Even our parents would not have approved of them going after it, much less letting me tag along.

"Well, to make a long story short, they did catch the horse, and each of them tried to see how long they could stay on his back. By the time both of them had been thrown several times, I figured the horse was getting tired, so it would be safe to show myself and jump onto his back before the boys could stop me. Which is exactly what I did. We were all used to riding bareback sometimes, so it didn't scare me as much as it should have.

"Anyway, when I jumped on, the sight of me up there startled my brothers so badly, they both jumped and yelled, which spooked the horse. He reared and pulled free of the rope they had tied around his neck. He ran like the wind with me clinging to his mane with shaking fingers. I'm not really sure how far he went because he threw me long before he stopped running. I landed hard, belly down, directly on top of a huge, jagged rock pile."

There was a gasp from the other side of the table, but Katie seemed not to hear it.

She continued her story. "King was afraid to move me, so sent Bob home to get help. It seemed to me that every ranch hand and some of the neighbors came barreling over the range in their pickups or on horseback. Anyway, as Dad and the guys tried to gently lift me off that rock, the pain made me faint. I was told later that they put me in the back of Dad's truck, where Mom had had the sense to throw in an old mattress out of the bunkhouse. I was told they got me in to the hospital in record time, but I was unconscious from the pain and loss of blood when we got there. I was rushed into surgery and was not expected to make it through. When I finally came to, Mom told me that the rocks just missed my kidneys and bladder but had so damaged my uterus, ovaries, and part of my liver that they had to be removed. At nine years old, that did not mean much to me then. It does now. Of course, I told Russell all of this when he first suggested we become engaged. He said he loved me enough to marry me anyway, so we went ahead and tied the knot. But I still wish I had not been so foolish back then so I could give him a child now."

Abbi had been quiet during the telling of the story. Now she came around the table and took Katie into her arms.

"I can't begin to imagine the pain you must have been in. That was a horrible accident for anyone to have, but especially one so young. It does explain why both of your brothers are so protective of you. They don't want to see you have to go through anything like that again."

"Yes, and I think both of them still feel a little guilty that they didn't try harder to stop me from following them that day. Not that anything short of locking me up would have done the job. They are right, I am too stubborn for my own good."

"Yes, you are stubborn, but sometimes stubbornness can be a good thing. You just have to know when to back down."

"Something I still need to work at doing. Say, enough about me. Let's go on over, and I'll see if Sam wants to go with me on the way to the grocery store. She seemed to enjoy watching the training session the last time we went. I'll carry Rona while you get your sewing and Ren."

When they entered the family room, it was to find all three of the other ladies with a project in their hands. Granny Edi was busy knitting another sweater for one of the twins, Sam was finishing up a couple of sketches for fabric design ideas, and Meli was jotting out caption thoughts for her latest photography book.

Katie said, "Good morning, all. Hey, Sam! Want to come with me? Jake is having some kind of problem with one of my puppies and has asked me to come over to talk about it. I thought maybe we could go there, let me try to fix the problem, then continue on to get those groceries you need."

Sam said, "Sounds good. I can finish these sketches when I get back. I'll work hard to have them ready for you to take to Phoenix Fabrics, Abbi. You leave when? Tomorrow?"

"I think that has been changed to the end of the week. Which is good, because on the way over here I got a call from Mr. O'Shay. He has a horse he would like me to come see. I'd like you to go with me, so whenever you can get off a couple of hours, we'll go down and check it out."

Katie and Sam left in Sweet Pea soon after that and were at the training facility in about twenty minutes. It took Katie almost that long to find Jake Finnigan. When she did, he called over a uniformed lady to take over with the dog he was working and motioned Katie and Sam into the snack bar.

As Katie and Sam sat down, Jake walked over to a man standing by one of the windows, then they both joined the girls.

"Hello, Katie, Sam. I'm glad you could come so soon. This is Dick Wilson. He has been partnered with Red, and that is why I gave you a call."

"Red!" Katie exclaimed. "But he was the most responsive puppy in that litter! I can't think you are having problems with him."

Mr. Wilson laughed, then said. "Not so much of a problem, really. He has just made it very clear that he doesn't want to be a drug-sniffing dog. Weapons either, for that matter."

"Oh." Katie said. "But that means he is not what you need. He has flunked out of drug-sniffing school! Do you want me to buy him back?"

"Maybe, maybe not." Jake said. "You see; Dick has a five-year-old son who was born with Down's Syndrome. Jeromy and Red have become almost inseparable, and the boy seems to function better when Red is close by."

Dick added, "We were wondering if you would consider continuing your Companion Dog training for Red, and see if he would respond to that better than what we are doing now. I have tried every method we have and he shows no interest in sniffing out drugs. He will not even play the tug-of-war games with any real enthusiasm. What he does seem happy doing is helping my Jerry at whatever he wants to try. Jerry has gotten a lot more self-confident with Red at his side, and I think they would make a better team than me and Red in the drug area. If you agree to this, I will buy Red from the Agency, and keep the dog I am currently working with for a little longer."

"So you are saying that Red is not a complete failure? That he can still be useful?" Katie asked.

"Exactly." Jake said. "It is not uncommon for dogs to 'flunk out' as you put it. Some of them, like Red, just don't want to do this and let us know it. It's not that they are not smart enough to do the job. It's more like they are smart enough to know it is not the job they were meant to do."

Rick added, "Right. It's as if Red is telling us he would rather be a companion for my son than to sniff out that stinky drug stuff."

"Then let's bow to his wishes. I can pick up his training where I left off and see that your Jerry gets a very loyal companion. When do we start? And where?"

"Why don't I bring him to your kennel on Friday afternoon, if that would work for you?"

"Great. Let me start with just Red at first, then with both of them after I evaluate how much extra training Red will need. It shouldn't be much since he seems to have learned a lot on his own! However, I would like a list of what Jerry can and can't do for himself. Some children become very lazy and let the dog do more than is good for either of them."

The two men chuckled at that and Rick promised to get a list for her. The two ladies soon said their good buys and left to do their grocery shopping.

"There is something about that woman that bugs me." Jake Finnigan said.

"Katie?" She seems fine to me." Dick commented.

"What? Oh, no, not Katie. It's Sam. I just know I've seen her before, or someone that looks like her, but I can't remember where or when." Jake said. "No matter. I like both of them, and I'm sure it isn't important."

# Chapter Twenty

Si, Jenny, and their almost nine-year-old son Joel came up and settled into their rooms. His crew arrived a few days later, either for rooms at the hotel or in the campground nearby. The men bringing their wives had listened to them and decided to stay at the campground rather than the hotel, agreeing they would be happier there than around the noisy construction.

Jenny and Joel, however, were very happy living in their apartment. Jenny jumped right in with the furniture salvage project, even working on it when the other ladies could not be there. She and Joel took long walks and took their bicycles into Lakeview often. While it was getting too cold to swim, Joel still liked to play along the shore, and had found several 'treasures' there. Jenny had gotten to know one of the waitress' at her favorite café, and found out Amy had a son, Calvin, just Joel's age. They set up a meeting for the boys, and they all four formed a fast friendship, visiting each other either at the hotel or Amy's house after she finished work at the café.

With three work teams going, the repairs and rebuilding progressed rapidly. Doc's clinic had already treated several patients because of splinters, bruises, and headaches. He had been able to sell his house, had completely moved into his small bungalow and was very happy with his new life. The fact that Betsy had taken over the kitchen and fed him his favorite blueberry pancake breakfast every morning helped him adjust quickly. However, Jeff soon spoiled his happiness by telling him to cut back on the pancakes, and eat more foods that were healthy. Betsy said she would see to it.

King had flown his family back to Texas, planning to return for the Grand Opening in two weeks. Things were winding down with the first phase of the project and they were just about ready to start renting out the new apartments. The burned out half of the building had been cleared away and the exterior walls put up.

Thanks to the extra help from Jenny and flyers from Sam's advertising business, the salvaged furniture had sold well, and added several thousand dollars to the building funds, enough that they could complete the offices necessary to running the home once it was complete. Ideas were still forming about other steps, such as the outdoor swimming pool and the putting green, but Russell and King knew those things would take time and more planning. They were just glad to have the exterior work done before the first snow. Si and his people would be leaving the next week, and Russell had already sent one of his crews back to the village to start on the new barn at Melrose Farm.

However, that project was delayed for almost two

weeks because of bad weather. Rain every day, all day, and some high winds.

Russell, Doc, and Si were taking a break at the end of the day and having a cup of coffee in the new dining room when Jenny came in. She rushed up to Si and asked, "Have you seen Joel?"

"Not since lunch." Si answered. "Why? Do you need him for a lesson?"

"No, we finished his schoolwork this morning. He went out to play with Cal after lunch but hasn't returned. I called the boy's mother, but Amy said both of them came by her house, grabbed an apple, then left. That was about one o'clock. She is getting a little concerned herself since Cal has never stayed out so late. It's getting dark out there now, and I'm worried something might have happened to them."

Russell said, "Let's grab a couple of flashlights and start a search. They probably started playing down by the cove or in the woods and lost track of time."

After hours of searching and calling the boy's names until they were all hoarse, the boys had not been found. Jenny and Amy were getting frantic, and the guys were getting more concerned as time went by.

Finally, Doc suggested, "Listen, I don't want to frighten you any more than you already are, but I think the situation has gone beyond what we can deal with. I think it is time to call in more help."

Russell asked, "What do you mean, Doc? Call in the police?"

"No, not really. Not yet, anyway. Didn't your Katie sell one of her dogs to a Search and Rescue guy? Maybe she could ask him to come up here and help us find Joel and his friend."

"I'll call her right now!"

Katie reacted swiftly. She placed a call to Brad Phillips, told him what she knew of the situation, and asked if he could bring a rescue team to search for the boys.

"Well, that is not really following the usual procedure. We usually have to wait to be called in by the local officials. However, for you and your friends, I will bring Lady along with my Elsie and call this a training procedure. I can be in Lakeville in about twenty minutes. Ask the mothers to have something that belongs to the boys for the dogs to smell. I'm guessing I'll see you there?"

"Of course. 'Bye for now."

Katie then told the others what had happened. All but Granny Edi elected to go along to offer support to Si and his wife, and the other boy's mother.

Gathering in the living room of Doc's bungalow, Katie and the other ladies huddled in a corner sitting area, while the men gathered in the kitchen. It was hard to just sit and wait, but Brad Phillips had explained that having so many people along would actually hinder the dogs in their search. However, he allowed Katie to come along so she could see Lady at work.

It was almost daylight when Russell's cell phone rang.

"We have both boys." Katie said. "They are basically fine but it seems Calvin fell and has an injured leg. Can one of you bring a First Aid kit to the groundskeepers shed at the back of the hotel property?"

Calvin's Mom, Jenny, and Doc Simmons all jumped up and started for the door, Doc grabbing his medical bag on the way out. Russell followed them to guide them back to the shed, giving each of them a flashlight on the way.

Sam and the others started putting together food and beverages for when the boys and rescuers returned. They also discussed the fact that the guys had searched that shed earlier in the evening, but hadn't seen or heard anything to indicate the boys were there.

The rescue party returned in about an hour, with Calvin wearing a bandage on his leg below a badly ripped leg of his jeans. They all settled down with plates and cups. Then the questioning began.

"Okay, young man." Amy said to her son, "Would you please tell us where you have been all this time?"

Calvin took another sip of his hot chocolate, then said, "Well, right after lunch we took our bikes out to the campground to see if Joel's other friend was still there. He wasn't so we went to the park in Lakeside to mess around on the swings and stuff there. After that, we went over to the railroad to watch the trains, then over to Kelly's Creek to skip stones. The bank was slippery with all the rain we've had. I was skidding down the slope when my bike chain caught in my pant leg and I fell. I didn't think it was too bad so got back on my bike. By then it was getting dark so we headed home, but started talking about how we wouldn't be able to do any of those things anymore 'cause Joel had to go back to his other home. That's when we decided to hide until after his parents left and he could stay here with me."

"But why did you hide in that old shed?" his Mother asked. "Didn't Mr. Mayhew tell you it was dangerous to play in there with all the equipment and tools?"

Joel hung his head, then said, "We thought that if he thought it was so dangerous, he wouldn't want to come in there himself so he wouldn't find us."

Si exclaimed, "You didn't **want** to be found?"

Calvin spoke up, "Joel didn't, not until you and his Mom had already gone back to your home. He wants to stay here. We're friends!"

There was a stunned silence around the room.

Amy asked, "You really thought that hiding out would keep him here? That his parents would just leave without him?"

Both boys mumbled, "Maybe."

"Well!" Doc Simmons said, "I think this discussion is best left for later. Cal needs to get to bed with pillows under his leg, and I'm sure the rest of us are ready for some sleep as well."

To Cal's mother, he added, "I will make an old-fashioned house call later today, or you can take him to your own doctor. Whichever, that bandage needs to be changed."

"Umm, I can change it Doctor Simmons. Thank you for all you have done, but since my husband died, I'm afraid my budget will not stretch to cover house calls. I'll pay you for what you have already done, of course."

"No, you will not!" Doc answered. "I'm just glad I was around to do it. And, I will be out to see him tomorrow, no charge."

"I will not take charity, Doctor Simmons. Is there a way I can work for you to pay the fees? I was trained as a nurse, but there haven't been any medical jobs available here in Lakeside until you opened your clinic. Could you use a part-time nurse?"

"What a marvelous idea! Would that be alright with you, Russell?"

Russell answered. "Yes, but only if you make it permanent! We had intended to hire an assistant for Doc but have just not gotten around to it. You have saved us some time and the frustration of going over applications! When can you start?"

"Oh! That would be wonderful. I will have to give two week's notice to the restaurant where I work, but I could start any time after that. Thank you!"

Russell said, "Thank you! Neither King or I like the paperwork involved with the hiring process, so you are doing us a favor."

"Well, thank you again. And Cal, say 'Thank you' to Mr.

Phillips and his dogs. Even if you did not want to be found, he did you a service."

"Thank you, Mr. Phillips. Say, that was neat how Lady kept digging at that pile of mulch until she found Joel's foot. I thought we were so far under it nobody could find us."

"You are very welcome, son. And Lady was just doing her job. She likes finding lost boys. But that does NOT mean either of you can test her again. Understood?"

Joel said, "We understand, Sir, and we won't get lost on purpose again, but it is great how she did that. The next time you have to find somebody, can I come to watch her work?"

"We'll discuss that later. Right now, you need to get in bed."

The two boys followed their mothers and Si out, but the others sat back down, glad that it had turned out so well. Sam asked, "So it was Lady that actually found them? What about your old partner?"

Brad smiled and said, "Remember why I bought Lady? Because I knew my Elise was getting too old for this job. And with her much shorter Beagle legs plus her age, she just was not able to climb up into the loft where the boys were hiding. You all should know Lady was so sure the boys were up there she went up that vertical ladder as if it were a gradual slope! By the way, they heard you calling earlier today from the top of the ladder Russell, but they chose not to answer."

Doc spoke up to say, "I think the best part was you bringing Lady down that ladder! She must really trust you to be so relaxed while you carried her down backward."

"That, too, is a part of her training. We have to make sure our dogs can get out of some pretty tight places, and sometimes that means we carry them. She has been quick to learn the routine."

"So my Lady is doing well with her training! You heard about Red, I suppose."

"Yes, I heard about Red, and applaud his choice. You shouldn't worry about his so-called 'failure', Katie. It actually shows how smart he is. By rejecting the drug-sniffing in favor of being a Companion Dog, he is telling us he knows what is best for him. Be proud! And that goes double for Lady. She is absolutely amazing. Jake tells me the other two boys are doing well also, so you should not worry about any of them. Now, I need to get myself and my dogs home. Thank you for allowing them to invade your house, Doc Simmons, and for the bowls of water. Good night to all of you."

Katie walked out with him and offered her thanks again for finding the boys. As she waved goodbye, Russell and the others came out on their way to the cars for the trip back to the farm.

# Chapter Twenty-one

S I CALLED RUSSELL ABOUT MIDMORNING the next day. He asked if he could talk about what had happened the day before. After being assured that Si wasn't angry or placing blame on Melrose Family Construction for the incident, Russell agreed to drive up to Lakeville that afternoon. Not that he would have refused to talk anyway, but it helped to know Si had no hard feelings.

"Hey, guy!" Russell said when they met in the driveway outside the front door of the new Retirement Home. "I thought you were planning to leave today."

"Yes, well, that is what I wanted to talk to you about! Come on, let's sit in the Lounge."

The lobby of the old hotel had been enlarged, and now held not only a reception desk, a couple of elevators and public telephones but also groupings of easy chairs and tables, shelves of books, games, and puzzles. Becky brought them cups of coffee almost as soon as they sat down.

Russell said, "Becky, you know there is a "No food or drink" sign posted in here. We don't want your food service operation to end up being spread all over the Home!"

Becky answered, "Yes, I am aware of it. I put it there, if you remember. But since there are no residents around yet, and you two want to talk business, I will break my own rules this once."

When she had gone back to her kitchen, Si put his cup down and said to Russell, "Well, old friend, I have a favor to ask of you."

"Listen, after what you did for me when I left our business years ago, you know you can ask anything."

"Well, then, here goes. You heard Joel and Cal last night when they said they did not want Joel to leave here. Well, it appears Jenny and I don't want to leave, either!"

"What are you saying?"

"Let me back up a bit. I'm sure you remember the guy that was our biggest competitor when we were just starting out. He has gotten even more powerful, and more mean and underhanded in his dealings since you knew him. I have been fighting a losing battle with him for the two last years or more. Also, his wife has taken it upon herself to make Jenny's life miserable every time they run into each other. And I'm sure you remember how small that town is."

"Yep. Small minded as well as small in size." Russell said. "So tell me the rest of the story."

"Well, Jenny and I had a long talk after we finally got Joel in bed last night. We would both like to move my construction business, and if you are okay with the idea, we would like it to be centered right here in Lakeside."

"What! This close? That would be great! Why would you think I would not be okay with having you here?"

"We certainly do not want to take any work from you. I need to do some more research and see if there would even be enough business for me here. I will look for mostly small home jobs for the many retirees I understand would like to move here near the lake. I just don't know yet if there is a need for another construction company this close to yours."

"As you know, I started Mayhew Construction building single family homes, but that has changed gradually. Let's see, if I continue to concentrate mostly on commercial buildings in and around my village and over in the valley and you continue to build private homes here in this area, we would not be fighting each other for jobs. I think it would work out well. How long would it take to get your business closed down and moved?"

"We have a good amount saved that would last until I can get enough work to pay the bills. Some of my crew would like to stay also, mostly the unmarried ones that have no family to go back to. So, maybe a month to close down there and get the family settled here. And that is where the favor comes in. Jenny and I wondered if you would let us continue to live in that apartment until I can find some land and build our own house. We would pay you the rental fee just like any new tenant."

"I would have to talk it over with the rest of the joint owners, but I don't think there will be a problem. As you already know, this is a 'family run' venture and I will talk to most of them tonight. King is not due back for a few days, but I'll call him tonight anyway. As far as I'm concerned, I would very much like to have you here! We might even find a couple of joint projects again!"

# Chapter Twenty-two

THE IDEA PASSED WITH THE enthusiastic approval of all the family, and things settled down to a fairly normal routine. The new barn was completed, the four horses and the goats were moved in. Katie was happy that she did not have to maneuver around them anymore to get her car into or out of the 'garage'. Not much had been done to that end of the barn yet, just removing the partitions between stalls to make room for the two vehicles. Russell promised her to make it better as his time permitted.

As they were enjoying the evening chat in the family room one evening, Granny Edi asked if any of them had listened to the weather forecast. None of them except Jeff had, so she said, "The news station reported that an early, very heavy snow storm hit in the mountains at the upper end of the valley. Actual blizzard conditions, which is unheard of this time of year. I'm glad none of you have to go that way any time soon."

They all agreed on that, saying they all had enough to keep them busy right here in their own village.

Will then turned to Russell and said, "Hey, Bro, now that 'Bradley Place' is almost finished and even has several retired couples moving in soon, and our new barn is complete, do you think we can get to work on fixing up the basement here? As you know, Meli and I leave for my dig in Copenhagen just as soon as it gets warm enough, and I would like to see most of the recreation room finished before we go."

"Ah, yes. I've been meaning to talk to you about that. I have both of my crews working on that new office complex north of the village, but that should be finished by the end of next week. We can start on your renovation's any time after that. Even earlier if we want to do some of the work ourselves."

"Super! Maybe we can start by getting that old furnace out of the way. Meli wants that room as a play space for all the kids we don't have yet! I just want the thing gone before it rusts out so badly we will have to take it out in small pieces. Can we maybe start on that this weekend?"

Jeff said, "Don't count on us to help this weekend, guys. I have to go into the city for a medical conference and Sam is coming with me. We'll be glad to help any other time, though. And don't worry, Granny Edi. We will be going the other way, so we will not get in the snow. Anyway, there was supposed to be more rain too, so maybe that melted the snow so it didn't get too deep."

Russell said, "Not having you here right now is not a problem, Jeff. There isn't much room to work behind the furnace anyway, so it is probably best if just Will and I tackle it by ourselves. We can..."

Just then, Katie's cell phone rang. When she answered, she listened for a few minutes, then her face lost all color, and she gasped, "Oh, no! Yes, I can come right away." and she quickly got to her feet.

# Chapter Twenty-three

SHE TURNED TO THE OTHERS and said, "That was Brad Phillips. The dam at the lower end of the reservoir over in the valley sprang a leak. With all this rain we have had lately, they are afraid it is going to break down completely and they need to evacuate some of the people downriver. He and his dogs are being called in now, just in case they have to do some rescue work for those not able to get out in time if the whole dam goes. He wanted to know if I would like to come over to help man the first responder tents, handing out coffee and sandwiches, and a central location for the rescuers, that sort of thing. Anyone else interested in tagging along?"

Everyone said they would go, including Granny Edi. She said she could hand out sandwiches as well as anyone and she wanted to be where the action was. Jeff grabbed his medical bag, and they all piled into cars to head over to where Brad had said the rescue headquarters tent would be. They arrived just in time to hear that the worse had happened. The rain on top of all the snow in the mountains had backed up behind the dam and the leak had gotten steadily worse until the entire dam had given way. Several homes had already been washed away, and more were expected to go at any time. Brad soon came by to grab a cup of coffee and told them that he and his dogs had helped bring in three people who had been stranded on their roof.

As he told Katie, "No real Search and Rescue yet, thank goodness. Just helping people get out of the water, and so far, everyone seems to be accounted for. We will have to see how it goes as the water recedes. Lady, stop making a fool of yourself and let's get back to work."

When Lady had seen Katie in the tent, she first looked at Brad pleadingly, and when he nodded his head, she had run over to Katie and almost bowled her over with an enthusiastic greeting. Katie had been giving the dog a good scratch behind the ears and murmuring loving endearments to her ever since. At Brad's emphasized words 'back to work', Lady gave Katie one last lick on the cheek and followed Brad out of the tent.

Several hours, many cups of coffee and dozens of sandwiches later, things were slowing down. Katie and her family were standing just outside the volunteer tent having a cup of coffee themselves and talking to some of the other volunteers. All of a sudden, a very wet golden retriever came running at full speed toward the group. Katie only had time to recognize Lady before the dog put her paws on Katie's shoulders and thrust a bundle of wet rags in her face. Instinctively, Katie grabbed the bundle, losing her coffee cup in the process. Just then Brad came running up.

"I don't know what has gotten into that dog!" He said as soon as he could catch his breath. "We were making our way back here, thinking the job was finished. Suddenly, Lady takes it into her head to plunge into the river again. There was a small house that had been swept off the foundation and was floating down the river. She swam out to it, jumped on the roof of the porch then into an upstairs window and disappeared for about ten minutes. She came back with this bundle of rags in her mouth, raced right past me, and came galloping back here.

"I am so sorry, Katie. She has gotten you all wet with those rags. I have no idea why she thought they were so important, and would not listen when I called her. I also know one of the first things you teach your puppies is that they do not jump up on people. What is wrong with her?"

"It's alright, Brad. I'm sure she had a good reason. Down, Lady."

Lady quickly sat at Katie's feet, looking up at her as if to tell her something. With the dog out of the way, Katie could now lower her arms a bit, and as she did so, the bundle of rags moved!

Katie carefully unwrapped the first couple of layers of blankets and exclaimed, "Oh, my gosh! It's a baby! Brad, Lady has rescued a baby! Look, these aren't rags. They're baby blankets tightly wrapped around a baby! She didn't have time to say more before there was a horrible sound of retching, and then a fountain of water erupted from the baby's mouth. Then another retching and ejection of water. Then the baby took a deep breath and let out a long cry. Katie instinctively raised it to her shoulder and started patting it's back and making soothing noises. The baby soon stopped crying and began to relax in Katie's arms.

"Holy Geronimo! You are right! Lady, I will never doubt you again! You somehow knew to search a little more. I wondered why she was trying to hold that bundle so high to keep it out of the water. Now, we need to find the parents of this little one. Katie, will you bring it this way, please? Let's go over to the hospital tent and see if the parents are there."

# Chapter Twenty-four

THEY WERE NOT. NOR WAS there any record of them having been there. However, one of the volunteers recognized the baby, and told them the names of the parents and said she thought the baby's name was Susan. She gave them a dry blanket for the baby and they went over the whole area, asking questions and finally, reluctantly, went to the temporary morgue. There they asked the attendant to check his records. Sure enough, both parents had been found downriver, along with several others, drowned and floating in the swollen river.

They went back to the volunteer at the hospital tent to see if she could give them any more information. She started crying when they told her about the parents. She introduced herself as Elizabeth Summers and told them that she worked at the hospital where the baby had been born only a week before. That is where she had first met the parents and had been on duty in the delivery room when the baby was born. That was why she recognized her, and one of the blankets wrapped around her, so quickly. The hospital always gave newborns a blanket when it left to go home and it was that blanket that had given her the clue as to who the baby belonged to. She also said that as far as she knew, there were no other relatives of either parent listed in the hospital records. Then they asked if she could go over to identify the parents as they did not have any identification on them when found, and were being recorded based on guesses by the volunteers.

At that moment, Jeff walked over to see what was going on. He had been so busy treating the injured survivors he had not seen Katie and Brad enter the tent. After Katie told him all she knew, he said, "Right now that baby needs to be gotten out of the rest of those wet clothes, warmed, and fed if possible. Let's see what we can do to get those things taken care of."

"Of course!" Katie said. "Brad, would you mind going to the rest of my family and tell them where I am? They must be getting pretty frantic about my sudden disappearance, but I feel I have to stay here with little Susan."

"Yes, I can do that. Then I really need to get my dogs home and taken care of. They both worked hard today, and are wet as well. Call me later and tell me what happens with the baby."

Elizabeth, Katie, and Jeff worked together to get the baby warm and fed, using extra rescue team blankets and diluted milk from the coffee tent pored into a sterile glove with a small snip in the tip of the little finger. After that, Jeff pronounced Susan as healthy as could be expected, although he was pretty sure Lady could not have held her high enough that she did not get some of the river water in her lungs. He told Katie that since there was no one else to care for Susan, it would be up to them to get Susan to the hospital as soon as possible so he could do some x-rays and other tests.

When Katie got back to the others, they all agreed that was the right thing to do. Katie, Russell and Jeff started for the hospital with Susan and the others went back home.

When they arrived at the emergency entrance, Jeff took the baby and hurried inside, telling the others, "I will take care of Susan but you will have to fight with the admissions staff! Sorry."

And what a fight it was. They could not provide any insurance information, they did not know her address, the story that a dog had brought the baby to Katie was met with stunned laughter, and they were told that the police would have to be called, practically accusing Katie of stealing the child.

Thank goodness, Jeff came back about that time. As soon as he was recognized as the Chief of Staff for the hospital, the entire atmospheres changed.

"Dr. Barlow! Are these people with you?"

"Yes, they are! You and your staff need to show them a little more respect. They are trying to get help for a survivor of the flood over in the valley, and they certainly do not need any more hassles from this office. I know the whole situation is a bit unorthodox, but believe me when I say it will be handled in the proper fashion, just not at the moment. Right now, they will come with me to the children's ward and see Baby Susan."

As Katie and Russell turned to get on the elevator, they heard Jeff tell the admitting clerk, "I will talk to you tomorrow. I don't think this was handled properly, even if they had not been my family. If this is the standard way to treat people coming in here for emergency help, we need to discuss a new procedure. Meet me in my office tomorrow at nine."

As they were riding up to the third floor, Jeff spoke quietly to Katie and Russell, "We have her in the children's Intensive Care Unit right now, so she can be constantly monitored 24/7. I have ordered a portable x-ray and antibiotics to fight any infection she might have picked up from the muddy water. Since you told me that the blankets were completely soaked when she was thrust into your arms, I can only assume she was completely under water at some point, in spite of Lady's care to carry her as high as possible. For how long she was covered with water is anybody's guess. We know she did not drown, but we can't know how long, or even if, her brain was without oxygen. You told me she threw up water twice, so that's a good sign. We were able to suction out more water from both her lungs and her stomach, but that may not be enough. Suctioning lungs, partially on someone this small is tricky. Too little suction and you get nothing, too much and you can collapse the lung. Right now, we have done all we can until the x-rays are done and the results of the tests

I ordered come back from the lab. She was given a little formula, and now appears to be sleeping normally."

When they arrived it the ICU, Katie and Russell were able to see the tiny baby behind a glass window with a nurse checking some of the tubing going into Susan's arm. Katie almost whispered, "Will she live, Jeff?"

"I wish I could give you some guarantees, Sis, but we can only wait and see. Let's just let her sleep for now and go take care of that paperwork as best we can. Unfortunately, my staff was right on one thing. The police should be notified, or at least Social Services."

A Social Services agent arrived at the hospital while they were still trying to sort out which of the admission forms they could fill out with the scant information they had. Introducing herself as Alice Niemeyer, she listened carefully to the story and took copious notes. She was very helpful with the questions on the forms and told them what answers would satisfy both the hospital and Social Service protocol in a case like Susan's. She also told them that her agency would contact the hospital where Susan had been born and get their records for her, explaining the agency was more likely to obtain everything than if one of them requested the information.

When all the forms were finished, Russell asked, "What now? Will she be allowed to stay here until we know she is recovered?"

"I think that can be arranged. That will also give us a chance to locate a foster home willing to take an infant."

"Foster home?" Russell almost choked on the words.

"Why, yes. If she has no family, she is now a ward of the state, and will either have to go into an orphanage or be placed in a foster care facility."

"Why can't I take her home with me?" Katie asked, "Russell, would you mind if we did that?"

When he shook his head to indicate he would not mind, Ms. Niemeyer thought for a few minutes, then said, "You know, that just might work. I know we are short on any kind of foster care homes just now, and of course, the nearest orphanage is full. I'll see what I can do to name you two as her temporary foster parents until an opening comes up." Turning to Jeff, she said, "Please let me know when you think Susan is ready to be discharged and I'll handle her case from there."

They shook hands all around, Ms. Niemeyer left, then Katie asked Jeff if she could go see Susan again. When they got back to the ICU it was to find Susan wide awake, being rocked and sung to by one of the nurses.

"I just couldn't help it! She is so sweet. Oh, the x-rays are back and most of the lab results are in. They are all noted in her chart."

Jeff excused himself to go read Susan's chart and the nurse handed Susan to Katie, who immediately sat in the rocker and began to sing. The fact that Russell winced at her off-key tune didn't bother her a bit. Susan seemed to like it and that was all that mattered.

Jeff came back smiling. "Well, Sis, throwing up all

over you seems to be just what Susan needed! According to the x-rays, there isn't enough liquid left in her lungs to worry about. The body will now take care of itself on that score."

"That is really good news, Jeff." Russell said. "When can we take her home? If Social Services will let her come with us, that is."

"Not so fast, Bro. What we have to worry about now is infection and I'd like to keep her here for a few days to treat anything that might show up. Plus, I'd like a neurosurgeon to examine her. I'm still concerned about how long her brain might have been oxygen starved. I'd say the day after tomorrow at the earliest. Why don't you guys go on home now and rest? She will get the best of care, you know that. You can come back early tomorrow. I have to stay and check on another patient and do rounds. Please ask Sam to come for me in about two hours."

When Katie and Russell got back to the farm Katie went directly up to their bedroom to shower and put on clean clothes. Russell went into his home office to make a few phone calls. Then they went over to the family room to bring the rest of the family up to date on what had happened. In the middle of that conversation, Russell's cell phone rang. When he answered, he asked the caller to wait just a minute, then went outside.

His caller was Jessie Davis returning his earlier call.

"What's this about you wanting to adopt a baby? I

didn't know you and Katie were even thinking about that."

Russell told her what had happened, then asked how hard it would be for Katie and him to adopt Susan.

"Russell, much as I would like to help you with this, my training is in Real Estate Law. However, one of my partners has handled several adoption cases. Let me see if I can get in touch with him. I'll call you back."

Russell went back into the house smiling. He got himself another cup of coffee and had just sat down when he received another call. This time when he answered, he stayed put and just listened. Then he just smiled and handed the phone to Katie. The others could hear Abbi from across the room.

"Lady brought you a baby! Oh! That's wonderful! Can you keep her? Roll one of the twin's cribs over to your house, and use anything else you need. How long will she be in the hospital?"

"Hey, slow down, Abbi! I'm guessing Russell told you most of it and we will have to wait awhile before we know anything more. They have not even decided if we can bring her here. I'll let you know as soon as we do. What? Oh, bye."

She said she and King will be here to see Susan soon! "They really like any excuse to make use of that plane, don't they?"

# Chapter Twenty-five

ARRIVING AT THE ICU THE next morning, Katie went directly to Susan's bassinet and picked her up, moving carefully around the tubes cluttering the space. She had barely sat down in the rocking chair when Jeff and Doc Simmons came in.

Jeff spoke first, "I hope you don't mind me calling in a second opinion. Doc has had much more exposure to infants than I have, so I wanted to see if he could find anything I might have missed."

"I have already checked her over, and read her chart." Doc said, "I don't think there is any more to be done right now. As Jeff told you yesterday, infection is the big worry now, along with the oxygen starvation. Nothing has shown up yet, but keeping Susan another day wouldn't hurt. Based on my many years here, I am also going to recommend you talk to Ms. Niemeyer and ask her about having her agency cover the bills so far. It has been done in the past, so should work for Susan as well."

As Katie continued to rock Susan, the three guys moved out of the ICU and stood talking just outside the door. She couldn't hear what they were saying, but everyone parted with smiles on their faces, so she figured it was nothing important.

Doc Simmons left to go back to the lake but Jeff came back in to chat a few minutes and was just leaving when he heard himself being paged over the speaker system. He waved to the others and went to his office. There, Ms. Niemeyer and another man with a briefcase, who she introduced as James Cameron, another Social Service worker, were sitting in front of his desk

"Sorry to interrupt your work day, Dr. Barlow, but I thought you and your friends would want to hear this as soon as possible." Mr. Cameron said as he pulled out papers from his briefcase. "Ms. Niemeyer has explained the request to place one infant named Susan into the temporary care of a Mr. and Mrs. Russell Mayhew. These papers would allow that to be done, provided that couple meets the requirements of our agency."

"Exactly what would those requirements be?"

"Simple, really. They would have to submit to a home visit from our agency before the infant is placed with them, provide a separate bed for the infant while she is in their care, make her available for a home visit by Ms. Niemeyer at any time, and swear to bring her into court whenever a final placement of said infant is to be made. We would like to get these papers signed today if possible. Do you know if the Mayhews' would be available? We would also like your signature as a witness to the story of how the infant came to be known to all of you."

"I'll be happy to sign those papers as a witness right now, and both Mayhews are in the ICU visiting with Susan, but I can let them know you are here. But before I contact them, there is something you should know. As far as we could find out in this short time, there are no living relatives for this baby. That being the case, when I spoke with Mr. Mayhew earlier today, he indicated he would be interested in adopting little Susan, although he has not broached the subject to his wife yet. He doesn't want to get her hopes up if this can't work out for some reason. How can we make sure that it does?"

The two agents looked at each other and smiled. Then Mr. Cameron said, "Looks like your instincts are right again, Alice." Turning back to Jeff he said, "We had anticipated that, based on Ms. Niemeyer's observations yesterday. I can tell you this much, we would love for that baby to be adopted by loving parents, but there is a lot that has to happen first." Counting on his fingers he said, "Assuring the courts that all avenues have been covered to find any relatives, and if one is found, getting their permission and papers signed giving up any claim to the child, assuring our agency that this actually would be a loving couple and the best possible placement for the child, checking out the environment in which the child would be raised, and on, and on, and on. The whole procedure could take months. Would your friends be willing to keep her that long, knowing that she may have a relative that could take her away from them? You see, that is where the usual Foster Care family is a better choice. They know from the start that the child may not be with them for very long. That is something your friends will have to discuss at length. In the meantime, she can go home with them for a few weeks as soon as she is dismissed from ICU. They can let us know what they decide about a longer custody stay after they have talked it over."

Katie and Russell came down from ICU, happily signed the papers allowing them to take the baby home with them, and agreed to a home visit the next morning. Everyone said their goodbyes, Jeff went off on other hospital business, and the Mayhews' went back to the ICU to give Susan one more hug.

When they got back to the farmhouse, Katie was so excited she couldn't sit still. They all had a quick lunch, then went over to her house to set up a temporary nursery and get ready for the home visit.

Will and Russell moved one of the cribs from Abbi and King's side of the building, and the girls rearranged Katie and Russell's bedroom so the crib could be in with them at first. That would give them time to fix up one of the several spare rooms Russell had built on their side when he turned the barn into a home.

Ms. Niemeyer arrived promptly and was given a tour of Katie and Russell's home including the Cole's apartment on the other side of the kitchen and the Mayhew Construction downstairs. Then they took her through the connecting door into the family room and introduced her to the rest of the family. They had a cup of coffee and one of Granny Edi's peach turnovers, then she left to file her report. Katie and Russell left soon after to visit Susan and find out how she was getting along.

Jeff found them in the ICU where both of them had a baby on their lap. Russell looked a bit sheepish as he told Jeff, "This little guy looked kinda' lonesome. He was the only other baby in the room at the time, and I just wanted something to do while Katie rocked Susan."

"And that's a good thing. Don't let me stop you. I just came up to tell you two I put in a call to Social Services this morning to let them know Susan can be discharged today. Ms. Niemeyer had just turned in her report on the home visit and they said it is cleared for you to take the baby home with you whenever she is ready to go."

Katie was smiling from ear to ear, and quickly got out of the rocker and started for the door.

"Wait up, Sis! I have to do one last exam and sign the discharge papers, then you can go. Sam called and told me that you have borrowed all the crib sheets and baby clothes you will need for awhile, but said to remind you to pick up diapers and formula on your way home. She also remembered to put one of Abbi's baby car seats in my trunk this morning, so we can get that when we go downstairs. I couldn't let you take her without it, you know. The neurosurgeon was in this morning and said he could find no evidence of brain damage at this time, but wants to do regular check ups for at least the first year. All of that will have to be passed on to Ms. Niemeyer. Now, please put Susan back in the bassinet so I can listen to those lungs one last time, then we'll get you out of here."

Doc Simmons came over to help celebrate with them that evening and was very pleased to see Susan so healthy. "But, as I'm sure Jeff has mentioned, she needs to have a check-up every week until we are sure there are no lingering infections in her lungs. Jeff, my guess is you prescribed some baby vitamins?"

"Yes, both vitamins and a mild antibiotic. Both as liquids so they can be added to her formula bottle. We also need to find a pediatrician for her, as I really should not be treating a family member."

Katie had been absorbed in holding Susan close and talking to her quietly. A Jeff's words, she jerked up and said, "Family member! Could she be that? Could we actually make her a family member? Russell, would you want to?"

Russell got up from his favorite chair and came to sit by her on the sofa. Putting his arm around her he said, "I wasn't sure you wanted to think of adopting Susan. The thought had crossed my mind and I have already called Jessie Davis to see if she can help. But to answer your question, yes, if Susan has no other family, I would very much like to adopt her. If you remember, I told you when we first got engaged that I had been in foster-care for several years. I would not want that for Susan.

"Really, Russell?" Katie was bouncing with excitement. "Oh, I so wanted to do that, but I didn't know if you felt the same way. I think I fell in love with her as soon as Lady put her in my arms. Do you think that wonderful dog could tell the future? Did she sense Susan should belong to me? To us?"

None of them could answer that question.

# Chapter Twenty-six

J ESSICA DAVIS AND HER PARTNER pulled out all the
stops and by working closely with Social Services,
the adoption was approved in record time. They were
just about to sign the final papers when Russell received
a call from Jessie.

"Russell, I am so sorry to have to tell you this, but a
relative of Susan's has been found."

"What! No! No! Katie will be devastated. Who is this
person? Do they want to take Susan away from us?"

"Hold on. You need to calm down. It may not be
so bad. Our team of investigators has located a distant
relative, a great uncle I believe, but we have not heard
back from him as to his wishes. I just had to call so you
can try to prepare Katie for the worst, if it happens."

"Yeah, thanks. You will let us know as soon as you
hear anything?"

"Of course! Bye for now."

Six days later, not so very far away, George Montgomery
rolled himself back into his room at the small hotel where
he had lived for the last ten years. Leaning over, he picked
up the pile of mail from the table by the door where the
cleaning staff always left it. He was muttering to himself

as he continued on into the living room area. "Leave town for three days and the stuff just piles up!"

Throwing away all the junk mail, tossing the bills onto the desk under the window, he stared at what was left. A very official envelope with a return address of Kendrick, Kendrick, and Meyers Attorneys at Law, located in a tiny village south of where he was now living. Wondering what a law office could possibly want with him, he cautiously opened the letter and pulled out the one page inside. After reading it several times, he broke into a big smile and rolled himself over to the telephone.

The time seemed to drag for Katie and Russell. They tried to continue with their daily lives but it was hard to do. Katie had given up working with her dogs. They seemed to pick up on her mood and didn't respond well to commands. Everyone at Melrose Farm was walking around on eggshells, waiting for the other shoe to drop. Katie just knew 'her baby' was going to be taken away, Russell was constantly worried about how Katie would hold up if this relative claimed Susan, and the others had run out of platitudes and assurances of 'not to worry'."

The family had just gathered for their after-dinner chat when Russell's cell phone rang. It was Jessie, and she asked if she could come over.

"I know it's after the business day, but for her best interest we need to get Susan's future secured as soon as possible. I will be bringing two other people with me that can do just that. Tonight!"

"Sure, come on," Russell said. "Let's get this over with."

It wasn't long before they saw Jessie's headlights turn into the driveway. Russell went out on the front porch to met them, and was gone longer than just greeting visitors should have taken. Suddenly, they heard him coming into the house from the back.

"Sorry I was gone so long. We took Mr. Montgomery around to the ramp I put up when we redid the back porch."

They already knew Ms. Niemeyer and Jessie, but the man in the wheelchair was a stranger. Until Jessie introduced him. "This is Mr. George Montgomery, the great uncle of little Susan."

The tension in the room became almost palatable, Katie hugged Susan closer to her, and Russell came over to put his arms around both.

George looked around the room at the hostile faces and broke into another of his big smiles.

"Miss Davis, let's not keep these good people in suspense any longer." Turning to the others, he said, "I am not here to take Susan away from you."

At that, there was a communal sigh of relief.

George continued, "I am seventy-four years old, confined to a wheelchair due to sever arthritis and live on a limited income. What would I do with an infant? But before I sign away any and all claims to her, I would like to ask for an addendum to the paperwork."

The family looked at him with shock written on their faces.

Before they could ask the questions he knew they must have, he continued. "I would very much like to have visitation rights."

At their surprised looks, he added, "You see, my father had a quarrel with his family even before I was born, and they did not communicate. Ever. After my parents died many years ago, I thought I had no family at all. Up until I received the letter from Miss Davis's office, I thought I was alone in this world, since my late wife and I could not have children. To find out about Susan was like an answered prayer. I would just like to see her as often as I'm able to get down this way."

In the silence that followed, Katie got up off the sofa, walked over to the old man and gently placed Susan in his lap.

"I think I speak for Russell as well as myself when I say we would love to have Susan's Uncle George in her life."

Russell said, "I agree one hundred percent." Turning to Jessie and Ms. Niemeyer, he added, "Do you have those papers with you? We will sign them right now."

# Chapter Twenty-seven

ABBI AND KING, WITH THE twins, and Bob and Ruth with their own son flew in for the christening. Si and his family came down from Lakeside, bringing Doc with them, and of course, Brad and Lady were there, Lady prancing around as if she knew she had done something great. Jessie and Ms. Niemeyer came and Katie had also invited Elizabeth Summers and Susan's Uncle George. Because of all her help in getting information from the hospital and helping in the investigation for the adoption, Katie and Russell had asked Elizabeth's permission and then named the baby Susan Elizabeth.

It was at this party that Uncle George told them that Susan was a family name going back many generations. His mother had, unknown to him or his father, kept in touch with the family occasionally, and he had a lot of the family history he would gladly pass on to baby Susan. His Mother had stored it in a box that he had finally dug of of the back of his closet after he heard about Katie and Russell's Susan.

Elizabeth not only brought a darling new outfit for Susan, but other things as well.

"First, here are the blankets she was wrapped in when

Lady found her. I washed them myself, so you could have them for her. After the water went down and we could get to the house, I grabbed a few volunteers and we were able to salvage a few things. The parents had rented it furnished but the owner released everything to us. The kitchen table and chairs and several other pieces of furniture were hosed off and sold at auction. Some of the clothing and linens were also washed and sold at that same auction. Here is a check for the full amount for a start on an educational fund for Susan. We were also able to salvage her crib and a chest of drawers full of baby clothes. Since they were upstairs, they didn't get damaged from the flood waters. And best of all, this was in one of those drawers."

She handed a book to Katie. When she looked inside, Katie started crying, then showed the book to the others. In it were pictures of both parents, before and after Susan's birth. Pictures of Susan being born. Pictures of the nursery they had prepared for her. And the typical baby book things, like her footprint just after birth, and a tiny lock of hair. There were also several pages of notes from both parents, telling the expected child how much they were looking forward to the birth and their hopes and dreams for their first child.

Katie said, "Oh, Elizabeth, this is wonderful. Thank you so much for going back to that house to save these things for Susan. I know she will treasure them when she gets older."

Russell added, "We will tell Susan about her birth parents as soon as she can understand. This book and the information from her Uncle George will help her feel closer to them. Thank you both."

As they were drinking coffee and eating slices of Granny Edi's latest baking effort, Granny turned to Alice Niemeyer and asked quietly, "Ms. Niemeyer, I've had a lot of time to think since little Susan came into our lives so suddenly. I was there handing out sandwiches when Lady brought her to Katie so I couldn't help but overhear discussions from some of the first responders. They were talking about how hard it was to have to tell the families of the drowning victims to claim the bodies and have them moved to a funeral home of their choice. Susan had no relatives, so there was no one to claim the bodies of her parents. What happened to them?"

"Oh, my! We don't usually have to deal with that question but thank you for caring enough to ask. Either the bodies are claimed quickly, or they are handled without anyone bothering to ask questions. In this particular case, Susan's parents were kept refrigerated either at a city morgue or at a funeral home for a certain amount of time, usually six weeks. Since they were not claimed by the end of that time, they were cremated, then buried in any local cemetery that would take them. Not in a 'mass grave' situation exactly, but without much in the way of markers."

"I see. Is there any way to find out where they are

and have them moved to a cemetery here in our village? I think Susan would like to have them where she could visit when she gets older."

"That is a very kind thought. Let me look into it and get back to you."

# Chapter Twenty-seven

ONCE THE EXCITEMENT OF HAVING Susan literally dropped into their family calmed down, Abbi and Sam drove down to see Mr. O'Shay and the horse he thought might be suitable for Sam.

"Good morning, Mr. O'Shay. It's good to see you again." Abbi said as she got out of Buttercup.

"Yes, and under happier conditions this time!" Mr. O'Shay said. "How do you like living in Texas? And in a castle, yet! I'm sure you never saw THAT in your future the last time you were here!"

"You are right about that! My life has changed so much since then. Which reminds me. I'd like to introduce one of my new 'sisters'. This is Samantha, or Sam as we call her. She is the lady who is looking for a small horse since she is just getting used to riding and isn't comfortable when she is on a tall one."

"Ah, yes. Good to meet you, Sam. Come right this way and I will show you 'Party Girl'. Miss Abbi, you called at just the right time. I seldom have grown horses this size, but she was brought in by the parents of her owner just after you called. That young lady has gone off to fly planes for the Air Force, so will not have time to ride much anymore, although she did competitive barrel racing with 'Girl'. They tried to sell Party Girl but didn't have any luck because of her small size. Their daughter was about your height, Sam, so fit well with Party Girl, but most riders like a bigger horse.

"Now, I need to tell you something before you see her. She looks to be an all-white horse, but don't be fooled by that. A lot of people think a solid white horse is bad luck, which is silly, of course, but in her case, you needn't worry about it. You see, she is half Welsh pony, which gives her the small size, and she is also half Appaloosa, which means she has black spots on top of the white. Her's are only on her rump and only show up when she is wet, so most of the time she looks to be all white but isn't. Can you live with that?"

"Ohhhh! A different kind of horse! I like that idea. Can I please see her now?"

"Of course! Step right over to the rail and I'll call her in."

Mr. O'Shay gave a sharp whistle toward several horses in the pasture and then they saw 'Party Girl' throw up her head and start trotting toward them.

"Oh, she is beautiful!" Abbi and Sam said at the same time. Sam pulled out an apple from her pocket and held out her hand. 'Girl' took it very daintily from her palm, chewed a few times, then butted her head against Sam's shoulder.

"Well, I think you have made a friend already." Mr.

O'Shay said. "I can assure you, she has been well trained. I believe she would be a good mount for you for years to come. She is only four now, so with good care, she will probably be around for a long time."

"Yes, I like her very much. How soon can we pick her up?"

"As soon as you like. She even comes with a one-horse trailer. Her original family is getting out of the horse business completely, so donated the trailer and all of 'Girl's' tack along with the horse."

Abbi said, "Sam, I don't think your Buttercup is heavy enough to pull a horse trailer. We will have to come back with a bigger car, or maybe even Russell's pickup."

"Yes, you are right. Mr. O'Shay, can I give you a deposit now, then the rest when we pick up my new horse?"

"No deposit necessary. I trust you two ladies. There is one other thing you need to know. Since she is white, she is more sensitive to sunburn than dark-colored horses, especially around the eyes. You'll need to keep a cream handy to prevent that. I'll give you a sample when you come to pick her up."

Abbi said, "I can't thank you enough, Mr. O'Shay, for all of this. We will be back soon to get her out of your way, so you have an open stall for any other horse you need to rescue. I know you don't like to have your spaces full, but you are doing such a wonderful thing by getting abused animals out of their horrible situations. Keep up the good work."

"Yes, I agree." Sam added. "Abbi has told us all about your operation here, and how you save these horses from mistreatment. If you ever need any publicity artwork done for flyers or advertisements, I would willingly donate my time. I am a Commercial Artist and have several contacts in the business, so I might be able to help you spread the word."

"I'll keep that in mind, young lady. Thanks."

Abbi said, "We really need to get back home now, but will be back as soon as possible to pick up 'Party Girl'. Thank you again."

Then Sam said, "I thank you too, Mr. O'Shay. See you soon."

# Chapter Twenty-eight

THE TALK IN THE FAMILY room that night was mostly about Sam's new horse and how soon someone could go pick her up. She also asked Abbi if she thought 'Party Girl' could get used to another name.

"I don't much like the name she has now. Actually, she reminds me of the beautiful white roses my Mother had years ago, so I think I would like to rename her 'Blossom'. I thought about 'Rose' at first, but then I remembered your Aunt Rose, Will. I wouldn't want to offend her by taking her name for a horse, so I settled on 'Blossom'. They all laughed, then Abbi said that it should not take too long for Sam's horse to get used to the new name.

Jeff said he would like to go along to say 'Hello" to Mr. O'Shay again, as he had stopped there while he was searching for Abbi after her disappearance. He also wanted to give him a sizable donation to help out with his rescue mission. He and Sam made plans to take his car and go down the following week as soon as they got back from the Medical Conference.

They had continued to talk for a few minutes when Katie's cell phone rang.

She ended the call, then told the others, "That was

Jake Finnigan. He has something to show us, so I told him to come on over. I hope it's not another of my dogs that isn't doing well."

By the time the girls had put on another pot of coffee and cut more slices of peach pie, Jake was knocking on the door.

Katie let him in and he came into the family room all smiles.

"I didn't think to ask on the phone but I hope your T.V. can handle DVD's!"

After being assured that it would, he continued. "This is footage from the security cameras at the airport over in the valley. It is evidence for a trial, so I can't leave it with you or show you all of it, but you were so concerned about your dogs doing well, Katie, I thought you would want to see this." He put in the DVD, stepped away from the T.V. and told them what was going on.

"As you can see, this is an overall picture of the large hanger used for freight. We routinely send one of our teams there to check on what is being sent out or brought in. There! That is one of our agents up on the left corner. And here, just coming into view, is her partner."

Katie exclaimed, "That's my Jinx! I recognize that white patch on his left ear!"

"Yes, now watch what happens next."

The agent walked along a row of crates and boxes with no reaction from the dog. She then led Jinx over to another row, and he began to sniff along the bottom crates. All of a sudden, he stopped, gave a growl, and started pawing at one of the crates. The agent called in the workers from the side of the room, motioned for them to pull out that one crate, then told them to open it. Inside, were several stacks of rifles!

At that point, the tape stopped, and Jake told them, "As I said, this tape is evidence in an upcoming trial, so I can't show you the rest. Katie, your Jinx not only found that one crate, but several others listed on the same manifest and awaiting shipment going out to a country which I can't name, but can tell you it is no friend to us here. They are all weapons stolen from a military base several months ago. We lost track of them and thought they had already been sent overseas somehow. This is the biggest weapons recovery in recent history, and it was all because of your Jinx. I expect he and his owner/trainer will earn some sort of medal for this, so look for it on the news as soon as the trial is over."

Katie said, "Thank you so much for sharing this with us, Jake. It seems that all my dogs are doing well in their new jobs. I am very proud of all of them."

They all settled back to enjoy the pie and coffee and a chat about the possibility of the agency buying more of Katie's dogs. After Jake had finished his refreshments, he got up to leave and was saying goodbye to everyone. As Sam came to take his used plate and cup, he gave her a close look, and muttered to himself, "It's something about the eyes. I know I've seen them before." To her he only said a cordial goodnight, retrieved the DVD from the television set and took his leave.

# Chapter Twenty-nine

EARLY THE NEXT MORNING, RUSSELL and Will went into the basement of the farmhouse to tackle the removal of the old furnace. They found it had rusted to the floor brackets and they had to take hacksaws to the connections to break it loose. Once that was finished, Will said, "Okay, I'll squeeze behind this monster and push. You try to find a good hold on the front and pull it away from the wall."

Russell grabbed the frame and Will braced himself against the wall behind the furnace.

Will said, "Now, on my three. One. Two. Thr... Ahhh!

As Will pushed against the furnace with his hands, his shoulders, back, and hips pushed against the wall. And kept going! The wall gave way and he fell down several steps before he could catch himself. Russell dropped his hold on the front of the furnace and rushed around to see what had happened. He found Will flat on his back inside a very large, very dark hole in the wall of the farmhouse.

With Russell's help, Will managed to stand up and assess the damage to his body. Not finding anything but a few scrapes and a large splinter in his hand, he and Russell began to look around at where they found themselves. As near as they could tell, it was some sort of cave, but with very obvious man-made steps leading down. How many steps and how far down they could not tell, as it was too dark to see anything beyond their outstretched hands.

Russell said, "Stay right here while I go get that LED flashlight out of my truck."

Will was happy to do so.

When Russell came back and shined the light into the space they found that the 'cave' turned out to be a tunnel and the steps went down another 10 or 12 feet. Going to the bottom of the steps and shining the light further, the tunnel kept going until it disappeared into the blackness beyond the rays of the flashlight. Just then, that flashlight began flickering and went out.

"Great!" Russell said. "I knew the batteries were about gone in this thing, but I wish they had lasted a bit longer."

"Why? So we would be even further along and have really been in the dark when they gave out? At least now we can make out the light back in the furnace room. Let's go find more flashlights. Then we can come back and explore further."

When they came to the hole in the wall. they both pushed against the furnace and moved it out of the way. Racing upstairs, they stopped in the family room to tell the others what they had found and to ask Granny Edi if she knew anything about the tunnel. She did not, saying that the discovery was a great surprise to her.

She said, "The questions are--Who dug it? and Why? This is a mystery we need to solve."

Will said, "I have lived in this house all my life, and Granny has too. I wonder why neither of us knew about this tunnel. Anyway, we came back to get flashlights so we can explore further. Do you want to come down closer to the entrance, Granny? You can yell encouragement to us as we go inside."

"Well, yes, I'd like that. Since you and King insisted on putting in that elevator instead of those steep steps, Sam, Meli, and I have gone down frequently. They clean what will be the new recreation room, and I have taken an inventory of the jars of preserves and things stored down there. Did you know there is still some black cheery wine way back on the top shelf?"

Abbi asked, "But how do you know what preserves and things are there?"

"Why, by the labels, of course." Granny Edi said with a chuckle.

"I don't mean to be rude, but you can't see them!"

"True, but I know that whole fruits, jams, jellies, and preserves have the label on the top of the jar, while the vegetable labels are on the side. Strawberry jam has the top left corner cut off, grape jam, top right, green beans, notch in bottom center, corn..."

"Okay, okay! I get the picture. I should have known you would have a system."

"You bet! Now, let's go exploring!"

While the guys searched out all the LED flashlights they could find, the ladies went downstairs and gathered around the large hole in the wall.

Katie, using the knowledge she had picked up from working with Russell, examined the hole closely. She said, "Granny Edi, it looks like this was a regular door at one time, with a frame, hinges, and everything. The hinges on the door gave way when Will pushed against it and is now lying on the floor inside. And look! Here is an old lantern hanging on a wooden peg inside the tunnel. I'll bet the guys didn't even see this."

"See what, hun?" Russell said as he, Jeff, King, and Will joined them.

"This old lantern hanging just inside the door. Will, can you use your archeologist skills and tell us how old it is?"

"Wow! My area of expertise is for a time way earlier than this, but I'd say it's probably one of the first kerosene lanterns made."

King said, "Let's put this in a safe place, and go see what else we might find."

Melissa backed away from the opening, then said, "You guys go ahead. I think I will stay here to keep Granny company and help her watch the babies."

Will walked over, put his arm around her, and said, "Had enough darkness in your life, Sweetheart? You need to put your temporary blindness behind you if you can, but I understand if you don't want to go into this tunnel right now. You might want to drag over a couple of chairs for you and Granny. Hopefully, this will not take too long but you might as well make yourselves comfortable." Giving her a kiss on the cheek, he turned on his flashlight and walked through the hole in the wall, closely followed by the others.

They had only walked about fifty feet when Russell stopped and called their attention to another short flight of steps with a door at the top. The guys had to put their combined strength into pushing the door open. With creaking hinges, it finally gave way and they were able to push it all the way open, only to be surprised by what they saw!

King was the first to recover, and said, "Well, this is certainly a different view of your garage, Will!"

While pushing the door open, they had moved a large shelving unit away from the wall and were able to walk into the garage housing Meli and Will's cars. Because it had once been a separate kitchen for the farmhouse, the building also had a brick fireplace next to the shelves they had pushed aside. It was now used as the only source of heat when Will wanted to tinker with the cars. Because he kept his tools lined up neatly on the shelves, they had added to the weight of the door they had pushed open.

Abbi spoke up to say, "I have read about 'Priest Holes' in novels. Do you think that's what this was?"

Sam said, "But why would they need to hide Priests here, in this country?"

Will said, "I'm thinking the tunnel was more likely a way of hiding from Native Americans. If memory serves, I believe I've heard Granny say that this building was the original cabin for the farm. If that is the case, her ancestors would have been at the mercy of marauding Indians from the tribes native to this area during that time."

"Wow! So much history here!" Abbi said. "I wonder where the rest of the tunnel leads. Did they have another way out, or just hide in the tunnel?"

Sam said, "Good question! Let's continue to explore."

# Chapter Thirty

THEY WENT BACK INTO THE tunnel and continued on the original course for what seemed like a long time, then came to another door. Again the guys put their weight together and pushed. It slowly swung open to reveal a large cave with other tunnels leading out of it.

Russell said. "Well, if my instruments are to be believed, we are now standing in a part of your new home, Sam."

"What! What instruments are you talking about, Russell, and what do you mean about my new home?"

"I brought along both a compass and an instrument that measures distance traveled. If the readings on them are correct, we are now in the same tunnel system we explored from the other side of the mountain Granny Edi just deeded over to you and Jeff!"

"Oh, that is exciting!" Sam said.

"Well, let's look around." King suggested. "Maybe there are clues to what this place was used for, if anything."

Shining their flashlights around they soon found evidence that the area had in fact, been used for storage. Wooden bins built against the walls still had bits of dried-up fruits and root vegetables. There were several old-fashioned barrels with a dusting of what looked like flour and cornmeal, and a small one with the word 'Coffee' written on the side. A wooden table on one side had dried herbs scattered across the top with other bunches hanging from a pole lashed to wooden supports.

Leaning his head around a bend in one of the small tunnels leading out of the cave, Jeff suddenly said, "Hey, you guys! Come over this way and tell me what you hear."

They all came closer and stood quietly for a few minutes, then they all exclaimed at once.

"Water!" "Dripping water!" "Sounds like water!"

Then Sam started moving forward as she exclaimed, "If this is going to be a part of my new home, I've got to see where this sound is coming from."

She had disappeared further around the bend when they heard her shout, "Jeff, you won't believe this!"

They all rushed to follow her, then came to an abrupt halt.

Sam grabbed Jeff's hand and said, "Look, Jeff! It's the same little pool we discovered when we were exploring the Crystal Cave tunnels. We were on the other side and did not see this tunnel from that angle."

"Wow! You are right, Sis." Will said. "Do you know what that means? Once you and Jeff incorporate the Crystal Cave and these tunnels into your new home, Meli and I can visit you from our house without even going outside! Katie and Russell too, just by coming into our house first. Boy! I wish I had known about these when I was a kid. Can you imagine how great it would be to play down here?"

Katie practically shouted, "Don't you dare tell Susan about these places! At least, not until she is much, much older. I can just see her trying to explore and getting lost down here."

"Well, this is certainly interesting!" Jeff said. "And something to think about later, but we know from our earlier exploring there was no exit from that end until the landslide opened up Crystal Cave. Granny's ancestors could not have gotten out going this way. Did they just use this cave for hiding in or something else?"

"The only way to find out is to keep going in the other tunnel." Will said.

# Chapter Thirty-one

S O THEY ALL FILED BACK and continued on. It soon turned a corner and went on in another direction for a good distance.

They finally came to another set of steps much longer than either of the first two, which led to a much larger cave. Here, the tunnel seemed to stop, and as they explored the walls of the cave, they discovered what looked like old sleeping platforms carved along one of the walls.

Then Will gave a shout. As the others ran to him, he reached out and grabbed a handful of vines. Pulling them aside, he uncovered an exit to the outside and sunlight poured into the cave. Walking through, he said, "Well, I would never have expected this! Why didn't I ever find it when I was a kid? Katie, we are now inside your Green Mountain!"

Katie ran out to stand in the sunshine and looked around. "Oh, you are right! Look over there. It's the end of your backyard, and I can just see the edge of your garage around the side of that hill."

"A hill that I don't remember being there! I know I have never seen that part of the property! How can that be? More of the mystery!"

"What is that in the other direction?" Sam asked as she came to stand beside them. "That isn't our village."

Will turned and looked at a distant view of a small town. "No, it isn't. That is the town where the university is located. You can see those buildings clearly if you ride to the top of this mountain and go around to the side that overlooks the valley. Just off to the left is the reservoir where the flood was that brought Susan to us."

King exclaimed, "This is amazing! And look over here, guys. This must be where the 'ditch' that runs by Granny Edi's house actually starts. It is a natural spring bubbling up out of the ground just outside the cave."

Will said, "If I remember correctly there are several more springs between here and your mountain, Sam. I always thought they were the only ones. This area of the farm was not used, even during Granny's childhood. She always told me not to try to farm this area as it was always too wet. Now I know why! It's full of surface water."

Katie had gone back into the cave to look around now that the sun was making the whole area brighter. She suddenly called out.

When the others got back to her, she showed them a small alcove in the cave, and several old wooden boxes stacked against the rock wall. When the guys pried up the lids, they found bundles wrapped in what looked like old oiled leather. Pulling one out and gently unwrapping it, Sam exclaimed, "It's a journal of some kind. The light is not good enough for me to make out the words, but it's full of a lot of writing."

King said, "Yes, the light is fading now that the sun is going down. I suggest we each grab as many of these bundles as we can carry and get back to Granny and Meli. I'm sure they are getting worried about us by now."

As quickly as possible, they retraced their steps through the tunnel. They had just passed the door into the garage when they heard Meli calling to them. Will answered her, and they were soon back in the furnace room of the farmhouse.

"Oh, Meli, do we have a story to tell!" Sam said as she came into the basement room. "But it is rather long. Where is Granny Edi? I know she will want to hear this!"

"You were gone so long, she and the babies were getting chilly down here. I suggested the three of them would be more comfortable waiting in the family-room and I went up to get them settled. I had just gotten back when I heard you guys talking."

Russell stated that he thought they would all be more comfortable upstairs. Everyone agreed with that suggestion. The girls went on up to put on a pot of coffee, and the guys moved over several sheets of plywood to prop against the wall to cover the hole to the tunnel.

# Chapter Thirty-two

ONCE EVERYONE WAS SETTLED WITH their coffee and cake, Granny Edi turned to Will and asked, "Well, what did you find out about what was hidden in our old house? And why I never knew about any tunnel in my own home?"

"Why you never knew about it is fairly simple to explain, Granny. That tunnel and all the other things we found were from a time way before you were even born, so it's no wonder you did not know about it. I'm not sure your parents or even your grandparents knew about it."

In her usual concise, straight-to-the-point way, Granny Edi just said, "Explain."

Will started with the obvious. "As you do know, that old furnace has been there for many, many years. I believe you told me once you had it put in just before my parents were killed?"

At her nod, he continued.

"Well, the wall behind it was put up many years before that. The hole that I fell through had, at some time in the past, been a regular doorway. The hinges had about rusted through and when I pushed against it to move the furnace, the whole thing collapsed. It had been plastered over and painted just like the rest of the basement, so we couldn't tell it was there. The entire tunnel was dug so it was all below ground ten to twelve feet for the entire length. We never knew it was there because it was deep enough that grass, and even a part of your vegetable garden, was growing on top."

"That's insane! Why would anyone do that? This just adds to the mystery!"

"Well, here is where it gets really interesting. Not too far from where we left you and Meli, we found more steps going up to another door. When we finally got that door open, guess where we were?"

Not waiting for her answer, he continued, "We found ourselves standing right in front of Meli's and my cars!"

At her gasp, he chuckled and continued. "Yep, we were in the garage! Or, rather in what was once the old kitchen, and before that the one-room cabin that was the first thing to be built on this farm. As we were coming back, King and Russell agreed with my assessment that this end of the tunnel looked as if it had been dug with tools that suggested it was put in at a much later date than the rest of it."

Russell spoke up to say, "We think that door was there in the garage, or cabin at the time, to be an escape route from attacking Indians during the early years of settlement in this area."

"Well, that would make sense, I guess." Granny Edi

said. "History books tell us that those were very violent times. But where did that escape route lead?"

Abbi picked up the story. "Because I was the last to go through the door into the garage, I was the first to go back into the tunnel, so I found myself in the lead. We kept walking a long way, until we came to another door. This one opened into a small cave that Russell tells us his equipment indicated was a part of Sam and Jeff's mountain."

"Equipment? Sam and Jeff's mountain? What do you mean?"

Russell then told her about the things he had carried in his pocket. Then continued the tale. "Not only a part of their mountain, but we actually found that small pool Sam likes so much. So the natural tunnels in their mountain connect with the man-made tunnels over here. After Jeff reminded us that there would have been no escape route out of the tunnels in that direction, we went back into the tunnel we had been in earlier."

Here Katie just couldn't help herself. She blurted out, "That tunnel ended in my Green Mountain!"

"What?"

"Yep." Jeff said. "We followed that tunnel to where it ended in a large cave near the base of Katie and Russell's mountain."

# Chapter Thirty-three

⟶⟵

THEN KATIE SPOKE UP TO add, "I was poking around inside the cave and found these bundles in a couple of old boxes. We opened one and found old journals. I can hardly wait to see what is written inside."

Will broke in to say, "Before anyone touches those bundles, and especially the journals, let's clear away these dishes and wash our hands. I almost feel we should put on white gloves like they use in museums, but I guess that is out of the question. All we can do is handle them as carefully as we can."

Meli said, "Yes, Sir, Oh Master of Antiquities, Sir! I'm teasing you, love, but I agree. As old as some of these things appear to be, we should try to protect them as much as possible."

"Agreed." Sam said. "Granny, since you will not be handling the bundles or journals, would you like another piece of cake?"

"No, thanks, Dear. I'm too excited to find out about these things to eat. I'd like to get this mystery solved!"

When they were all settled again, Russell spoke up. "May I suggest we carefully unwrap all of the bundles first and see if they all contain journals. That way, we can start with the oldest first, and maybe get a complete history of the tunnel and caves."

"Good idea." Katie said. "This one we opened in the cave has the date 1829. Let's see if there are any older ones."

There were several. After reading the dates on each one, they found that some of them were filled with the history of the family, why they had come to this country, daily happenings of the Melrose family and politics of the time. Those they put aside to read later. The journals containing information on the tunnels told them that it was, indeed, used to hide from several Native American attacks in the early years of Melrose Farm. These attacks were documented in detail, so proved to be very interesting.

Abbi asked, "Meli, Will, could you use your picture taking and book-writing skills to produce a book using the journals as the source material? I think that would be fascinating and a way to preserve this information."

Everyone agreed the idea was a good one, and Meli and Will said they would start right away.

In the later journals, they found a surprise! It became apparent that this generation of Melrose Farm members were very much Northern supporters! One of the women who had married into the family was one Edith Patrick from South Carolina. She and her Melrose family began using the tunnels and caves as The Green Mountain Stop on the Underground Railroad! The journals listed the names of all the refugees fleeing from oppression in the South and where they planned to go when they left Green Mountain. The Melrose family had closed up the entrance to the tunnels shortly after the Civil War was over and its existence had been forgotten over the years.

Katie was ecstatic to find out that someone else had called her favorite place 'Green Mountain'.

Granny Edi noticed Will had gotten very quiet on the subject. "I can hear you thinking, Will. What is it?"

"You always knew when I was lost in my own world, Granny. But yes, my mind is off on another topic right now. Well, not really another topic, but an addition to the newly discovered tunnels and caves. Since we now have even more of a connection between the families at the back of the three separate properties. I'd like to improve on it even more."

"What do you mean, Bro?" Russell wanted to know.

"Okay, let's play around with some ideas here. First, I think we need to run electricity into the tunnel, so we can light it just like any hallway in the house. I know that would make it easier for my Meli to walk through if she wanted to go to Sam's new house that way."

King answered the question before it was even asked. "Yes! We can use what I learned while building out the tunnels and caves in my Castle Rock. Shouldn't be too hard, just time-consuming. And lots of wire and LED bulbs!"

Will said, "Unfortunately, my time is getting pretty short with our departure for Copenhagen coming up soon and my current book to finish. But if we can get this first step done before Meli and I leave, I can put off the rest of the basement remodeling until we get back."

Katie said, "First step?"

"Umm, yes. What do you guys think of this? Say we run the electric lights not only into Sam and Jeff's mountain but also all the way into Katie and Russel's mountain. We could then turn that cave into what some people call a 'Summer Kitchen' and have cookouts and family picnics there. My mind even ventured into the idea of putting a swimming pool in the area between the bases of your two mountains.

"That land is useless as it is, and it shouldn't be too hard to turn the area into a spring-fed pool. The run-off could still come into the ditch by Granny's yard. After the pool is established, there shouldn't be any more water than there is now. But that could also be done later. I'd just like to get the tunnels lighted before we leave. Then all of you could make use of the cave for picnics while we are gone this Summer."

Katie grinned and exclaimed, "Oh, I would love to make use of my green mountain that way. With Susan to care for and my dog training, not to mention the bookkeeping for the construction projects, I will not be able to help much, but I'll do what I can."

Abbi added her willingness to help while her family was still in town, as did everyone else.

Granny thought it was a good plan since it would bring her 'grandchildren' even closer together. She was just happy to have the Green Mountain Mystery solved in such a happy way.

# Chapter Thirty-four

"BUT WAIT! WAIT! WAIT!" MELISSA was so excited she had jumped up and was pacing around in a circle, waving her arms. "Will, if we are planning to write a book on the first uses of the tunnels and caves, shouldn't I have a chance to get some pictures before you start changing everything?"

"Oh, you're right! I had forgotten about that book! I was so busy thinking about the future, the past was overlooked. Sorry, Hun, I certainly didn't mean to cut you out of your picture taking, and they should be a major part of the book. Tell you what, I will continue working on building the new recreation areas in the basement while you take all the pictures you need.

"Thank you! I will try to be as quick as possible so you guys can at least get some of the lights in before we leave for your dig."

"Uh... Meli?" Sam asked with concern. "Are you going to be okay carrying your equipment back and forth through those dark tunnels?"

There was a moment of silence. Everyone knew how Meli disliked dark places. Ever since her accident had left her temporally blind, she had a phobia about wanting her spaces well lit.

Then Abbi made a suggestion. "Why don't you forget the tunnels at first and take a horse to the big cave in Green Mountain? You can get there almost as fast by going through the pasture as you could by going straight through the tunnel route. Maybe by the time you finish taking all the pictures you need there you can gradually move into the tunnels. You will need a little light in them for your pictures anyway, right? Maybe not the permanent lighting Will was talking about, but at least enough to take pictures without using a flash."

"Oh, I like that idea! Thank you, Abbi. Yes, even in that big cave, I am going to need more light than the sunshine that comes from the opening. I will want pictures of the vines in place anyway, so extra light there will be necessary. As long as what lighting we use doesn't change the history of what I am taking pictures of, I'm sure I can work in those tunnels. I just don't want to have a bunch of electric wires showing up in something that is centuries old."

Will said, "Good thinking you two! We can start by digging out a saddlebag or two for your cameras, and you can work on the big cave first. By the time you finish in there, I should have the basement pretty much built out the way I want it, except for the finishing details. This way, we can both make progress."

Sam asked, "May I go to the cave with you, Meli? To

keep you company and maybe help move your equipment around, but mostly to look for design ideas. Those vines might make a lovely background for a fabric motif. There is also some moss growing just outside the entrance that I can turn into a small 'sprig' design for Abbi's costume fabric."

King said, "Well, Granny Edi, it seems like your tunnels and caves are going to benefit yet another generation of Melrose Farm inhabitants!"

# Chapter Thirty-five

ABBI, KING, AND THE TWINS went back to Texas the next day, planning to return in a couple of weeks. They would drive Abbi's camper/horse trailer with two of the Castle Ranch stock, and King promised to bring back the schematics for the wiring system in his home.

Sam and Jeff went to pick up Blossom, so the barn began to fill up. The goats seemed to like getting out into the 'back pasture' and have a go at all the overgrown vegetation. The fence between Granny's very wet backyard and that pasture had to be mended before the goats were allowed there, but it only took one day with everyone except Katie pitched in. She was just getting used to a baby running her life but was loving every minute of it.

Will searched around in storage cabinets in the old part of the barn and came up with two saddlebags he had used when he was a boy. He told the group that evening, "I used these when Old Man Barclay and I would pack a lunch and go exploring. He would come over on his pony early in the morning, I'd saddle up my pony and we would head out. Over the top of what is now Katie's Green Mountain, all the way down the other side, then along the base toward the next range and all over the trails there. Some were pretty good logging trails, but some were just faint animal trails leading nowhere. This was way before he became OLD man Barclay, of course. He was just plain Chris Barclay then."

Sam said, "You still have not asked him over so we can get acquainted. If he will be our neighbor on the other side, Jeff and I would like to meet him and his family."

"You're right. I should do that soon, maybe before Meli and I leave town." Then he turned to his wife to ask, "But to get back to your pictures, when do you plan to get started on them?"

"My goodness, Will! You sure seem anxious about these new projects! I haven't even had a chance to find out how much film I have on hand, how much more I will need, look into getting an additional battery pack for my digital camera, or lots of other things needed before I can even take the first picture. But you know all this. Why are you in such a hurry for me to get started?"

"Because I want to get started! I can hardly wait to really explore those caves and tunnels when they are well lit. Who knows what else is there that we couldn't see with just flashlights."

"Oh, in that case, why don't I go over to the big cave tomorrow and make notes on exactly what I will need to get the first shots. It may mean a trip to the camera shop in the village. Do you want to go with me, Sam?"

"Yes to both the cave and a trip into town. I need to pick up a few art supplies myself, so we can do both at the same time. Maybe even have lunch at Rosie's Place while we are there."

"Could Susan and I tag along?" Katie asked. "She will need more formula soon, and I would like to get it before I run too low. I'll even drive my new 'Sweet Pea!' It already has the car seat in it."

With those plans made, everyone soon went to find their beds.

# Chapter Thirty-six

"HURRY WITH YOUR SADDLING UP, ladies." Will told them. "I want to see if I can figure out why I never knew that cave was there. Going to it from this direction could show me how it stayed hidden all these years."

"But the sun isn't even up yet!" Sam complained. "What can you see this early in the day?"

"Won't know 'till I see it, Sis. Or NOT see it as the case may be. Anyway, while you ladies are busy inside the cave, I am going to scout around outside. Do you each have a flashlight? Yes! Then let's move out!"

"Well, Blossom, let's see how nicely you and I get along. This will be the first time I have ridden you for more than a few circles around the yard. Don't buck me off now, you hear?"

While Will's Spider and Meli's Eclipse led the way, Sam and Blossom slowly brought up the rear. Once they reached the pasture fence at the back of the property, Will stopped them.

"Look over toward where we now know the cave is and then beyond. Meli, tell me what you see."

Meli said, "I see the base of Sam's and Jeff's mountain,

across the back of our yard. Closer, I see the base of Katie and Russel's mountain. With a lot of tall brush in between. All that stuff you want the goats to eat down if they can even get to it. Didn't you say most of the back of our part of the farm is marshy because of all the springs flowing through it?"

"Yep, it's very wet back here. That's why I never played much on this part of the farm. Every time you step, you sink up to your ankles in mud. I would come here to mend the pasture fence when it was needed but did not spend much time here. There were too many other places to go and still keep my feet dry! Sam, what do you see? Use your artist eye to see details."

"Well, what Meli sees, of course. But when I look more closely, it seems to me that Green Mountain is split in two at the base. There is a big crack in it."

"Exactly! I never paid any attention to it growing up. I guess I saw just what I expected to see. Since the trail to the top is a lot further toward the other side of the pasture, I only came this close to fix the fence and was so intent on getting it done as quickly as possible, I didn't look around. But now, knowing there is a cave entrance in there somewhere, I can see a difference in the way the mountain slope meets the valley floor. Its almost like there are two mountains very close together. Or rather, one mountain split into two. They sort of blend together a short way up, so what's visible from a distance looks like one mountain. Now I know why I never knew about that cave. I never went close enough to find it! I'll have to tell Katie and Granny that we have just solved another Green Mountain Mystery. Let's tether the horses, climb the fence, see how close we can get to the cave from here."

"You lead and break a path, Will." Meli said. "I'm glad I only brought a note-pad with me today. Walking through all that underbrush with a camera would be tricky."

"Yeah, looks like some work needs to be done if you plan to get all your equipment through here. Rats! Guess I need to put off working on the basement a few days longer!"

"Jeff and I can help clear brush. Once he makes rounds at the hospital in the mornings, he can be pretty much free for a few hours, and I have no commitments right now, so we could work on cutting brush almost every day."

"You're on! But right now, let's get to that cave."

After pushing aside brush and climbing steadily for several minutes Will said, "Whoa! That proved to be rather easier than anticipated. Just a short hike up that depression between the two parts of the mountain gets us right in front of the cave. Once we get the brush cleared away, it will be an easy walk." As they came to the covering of vines that hid the cave entrance, he added, "You ladies go on in while I scout around here."

"Be careful with the vines, Sam." Meli said as they approached the cave. "I'd really like to snap a few pictures from this side before we disturb those vines too much."

"I'll hold them back just enough for you to get in and turn on your flashlight. Then I can come through."

With flashlights on, each of them went further into the cave.

Katie was talking to herself, "Hmmm, first thing needed is a tape measure! Or maybe one of those floodlight thingies Russell uses for his construction sites, then the tape measure. That way, I can see what I'm measuring. Now, if I set up the low-light stand here and the wide-angle camera here..."

Sam said, "You're doing it again, Meli."

"Oh, sorry. I keep planning my 'shots' out loud, don't I?"

"That's okay. I'm used to it after all these years. You've been doing it since our first year of college! It's just that right now I'm trying to concentrate on my own lists. One for the sketches I want to make for fabric designs, but another for all the cleaning supplies we will need after you take the pictures you want for your book. Just look at the accumulation of leaves and dirt that will have to be cleaned out before we can even THINK about bringing food in here! It's going to be a major cleaning job!"

"But I like my Will's idea, don't you? I think this will make a wonderful gathering place for the family on hot summer days."

Sam was giggling as she said, "You sound just like Granny Edi when she calls him 'My Will'. And yes, I think the end result is going to be worth the hard work involved. However, just thinking about it makes me tired!"

Just then, Will called softly from outside, "Hey, come quickly, but quietly. You'll want to see this."

Both girls went to the vines and peeked out. Barely a dozen steps away stood a magnificent deer. He just stood there for several minutes looking at them, then slowly walked off down toward the other side of the mountain.

Will told them, "I expect we will see lots of them here. They have not been hunted on these mountains for decades, so have no fear of humans. Are you two about ready to go back? I need my breakfast!"

# Chapter Thirty-seven

KATIE CAME THROUGH THE CONNECTING door just as they were finishing their eggs and bacon.

Will went downstairs to work on the recreation room, the three girls called "Goodbye" to Granny Edi in the family room, and went out to Katie's car. After a morning of shopping, lunch at Rosie's, and a short detour to check out the new play equipment added to the park, they returned home, tired but pleased with the day's accomplishments.

The after-dinner chat that evening was mostly about what was found at the cave.

Will started off by saying, "In order for Meli to use the pasture route, the brush will need to be cleared from the pasture fence to the cave entrance. Not a great distance, but that stuff is thick and tough. Any help would be appreciated. I would also consider putting a gate in the fence at that point, but it would be up to Russell and Katie since it is on their side of the line. I checked around outside while the girls were in the cave, and like what I see. Turning the place into a nice summer retreat will be fairly easy.

"The cave will certainly be cooler than Granny's

back-yard. Since her big tree came down, there is no shade to spread a picnic. Just outside the cave, there is a fairly level place that will be suitable for a few chairs if we want to be outside for campfires and such. Or just do a bit of star-gazing. As for the swimming pool I dreamed of, that may prove to be a lot more difficult. Just past the level part, the surrounding area is so wet and soggy, I'm not sure putting an in-ground pool would even be possible. Since that project would be completely in my part of the backyard, I can research what can be done without taking you guys from your own work, and it can wait until I get back from Copenhagen."

Meli broke in to say, "Will was also kicking himself for not discovering the cave back when he was a boy. We think we found the answer, and it took Sam looking at it from an artist's viewpoint to see how it was hidden in plain sight."

Granny Edi said, "Sam? What are you going to tell us about our home that we should have already known?"

"Ah, Granny Edi! It's not so unbelievable that you didn't know about it. As Meli said, the cave is almost 'hidden in plain sight', but only if you are looking for it. Will told us that the land is so wet he never played or explored back there. I'm fairly certain you and your sister didn't either. As he said, there were so many other places to play, you didn't need to go there for your fun."

Granny agreed by saying, "You are right about Clarissa and me not playing there! We went one time when we were very young. She sank so far into the muck, I thought I'd never get her pulled out. The scare from that added to the uh... 'displeasure' of our parents because we were somewhere we had been told not to go kept us from ever going back."

"Well, as I was saying, riding up to the base of Green Mountain as we did, away from the usual trail to the top, my trained eye could see what looked like a crack or division on the side of the slope. That 'crack' turned out to be the side of another, much smaller hill right beside the base of Green Mountain and slightly in front of it." Holding her two hands up with the palms together, she said, "If you think of this as Green Mountain, it appears as though eons ago, an earthquake or something split off one small part and it sort of slid down and away from the main mountain." Bringing one hand down and slightly away from the other, she demonstrated what she meant. "Just looking at it from even as far away as the back of the pasture, it looks like one mountain. Like our Crystal cave, the entrance to this cave is right between the two and was only exposed when the side split off, so it is pretty well hidden unless you are right in front of it."

Granny Edi said, "Amazing! I never realized just how much Ole Mother Nature had to do with the land, or rather what's UNDER the surface on this place."

Jeff asked, "What did you find once you got inside the cave?"

Sam said, "I guess that depends on which one of us

you ask. I saw a lot of sketching opportunities. Katie saw several photography options. She and I both agree though, the first items to take over there would be a tape measure so we all know what kind of space we will be dealing with, and some sort of lighting that runs on battery power. Just enough that she can get her pictures, but not enough that it looks 'modern'."

"And after that, as Sam pointed out to me while we were there, a LOT of clean up time!" Meli said. "Remember, there are a couple of centuries of accumulated dirt and blown-in natural trash, not to mention the soot on the walls and ceiling. They must have had their cooking fires somewhere inside the cave."

Russell said, "Hmmm. I wonder. Will, do you think some sort of power washer would work? Not too powerful, I would think. We don't want to damage anything or break off any of the rock walls with too much pressure, but just enough to get all that soot and dirt off."

"It might be just what we need, but do you have a generator big enough to handle something like that?"

"Sure. And the best part of using a power-washer is that the water would also help push out all the other dirt along with the soot off the ceiling and walls."

"I hate to curb your enthusiasm guys," Sam said, "and believe me, I'm all for making the clean-up easier, but I have a question. Where is all this water to run the power-washer coming from?"

"Oops. Guess we got ahead of ourselves again, didn't

we? There is certainly no water faucet even close. It would take a VERY long hose! And there is no way to reroute the creeks." Will said.

Russell said, "Wait now. Let's think about this for a minute. On some of my more remote building sites, I have called in big tanker trucks to haul water to us, both for my crew to drink and for when we are mixing cement. Why don't we look into the cost of a smaller one and just drive it to the back of the pasture?"

Granny Edi exclaimed, "Russell, you constantly amaze me with the ideas you come up with! I keep wondering what will be next."

# Chapter Thirty-eight

DURING THE NEXT TWO WEEKS, Meli worked almost every day in and around the outside of the cave, finishing up all the pictures she wanted from that end of the tunnel. Will finished the T.V. room and his billiard room in the basement. Since he had finished Meli's darkroom already, cleaning up the mess from where he fell through the door was all that was left to do.

The family was gathering in the family room one evening for the usual chat when King and his family arrived. All the men went to settle the new horses into their stalls, while the ladies put the coffee pot on and began slicing the raisin cake Granny Edi had made that day.

As they were getting out the china, Sam looked at Abbi and said, "You seem very happy about something. What is it?"

Abbi wouldn't say anything until they were all settled in the easy chairs and sofas in the family room. Then she pulled a letter out of her pocket and said, "I have some news I think you all might like to hear. King, be quiet! You already know what it is!"

"I didn't say anything!"

"No, but you were getting ready to."

King just smiled, settled more comfortably in his chair, and began eating his cake.

Abbi continued, "Now, listen up the rest of you. I received this letter about three days before we left Texas. Therefore, it is already almost two weeks old, so I think we need to act fast. Jeff, do you remember Mrs. Granger?" To the others, she explained, "She was my housekeeper and only friend when I was married to that creep. She and I have kept in touch with letters and some phone calls. Her nephew, Jude took care of the racing horses and was instrumental in pointing Jeff in the right direction when he came looking for me. When I sold the place, Jude went with the new owner of the horses to help care for them."

Waving the letter, she said, "Now Mrs. Granger tells me that owner has died and his son is getting out of the horse racing business, so Jude will no longer have a job. I was wondering if this family might consider hiring him? Even a part-time job would be better than no job at all, and he could probably pick up other work around here. I know he is a hard worker, and since he already knows and has worked with Star, Eclipse, and Spider I think he could get to know the others very quickly. There would be no race training needed, so I'm sure he would have time to take very good care of all the horses, as well as the other animals."

"Can I say something now, Sister Dear?" Jeff winked at Abbi, then said, "As far as I'm concerned, this is great news. Abbi is right about Jude being a hard worker. That 'creep' she was married to had a large barn full of Thoroughbred racing horses, and Jude was in charge of all of them. The few times I visited Abbi there and wanted to ride for pleasure, Jude was most helpful, as he was when I was asking questions after she felt she had to leave. Also, I couldn't help but notice that he kept that barn spotless and the tack in good shape. If this family hires him, I think it would benefit all of us. It would certainly take a huge work-load off our shoulders."

"And all I was going to say, dear wife of mine, is that I'm all for hiring the boy responsible for me meeting you."

A collective "Awww" from the group. Abbi grabbed his hand and he gave her a hug.

Then Katie said, "I wonder if he would be willing to help with my dogs? Now that we have Susan, I don't have as much time for their training."

Sam said, "We had better not ask too much of him right away. It might scare him off! I'll help with the dogs until we find out just how much Jude is willing to tackle."

Granny Edi said, "Sounds reasonable to me, but he had better learn to take care of my goats as well as Russell has been doing for the past several years. Can you teach him to do that, Russell?"

"Well, if he is as sharp as Abbi and Jeff say he is, I don't think that will be a problem. How long will he be able to continue in his current job, Abbi?"

Abbi looked down at her letter. After a few minutes,

she said, "He should be finished there by the end of next month."

Sam said, "Then I vote we get in touch with him and offer this job. Show of hands?"

After a unanimous show of hands, Abbi said, "Then if you will excuse me for a minute, I'll go call Mrs. Granger and find out how to contact him."

The family finished their cake and coffee, so Sam, Katie, and Meli started collecting the dishes. By that time, Abbi was back.

"She was ecstatic at the possibility of Jude working here." Abbi said. "She thinks he will agree and plans to call him herself to tell him to take the job. I gave her your phone number, Jeff. I will also give it to him when I call. Since you have already met Jude, I thought he might feel more comfortable talking to you."

"Sounds good. Why don't you call him right now? It's early enough where he is, so the time shouldn't be a problem. In the mean-time, I'm going after another piece of that cake! It was delicious."

"Don't you dare mess up another plate!" Sam called after him.

"I wouldn't think of it, Love. I'll just put it on a napkin and eat with my fingers."

At that comment, the other three men disappeared into the kitchen.

By the time they were back, so was Abbi.

As she walked into the room, she said, "He jumped

at the chance! He said he would love to come work for us and asked if we could recommend a place where he could rent a small room. I'll look into that while I'm here."

Katie spoke up to offer, "Why rent another room right now? Russell and I have those other two bedrooms vacant. Why not let him stay with us until he finds something else. He could have the whole top floor to himself."

Russell said, "Good idea, Hun. That way he and I can talk in the evenings about what he has to do for the goats. If you remember, sheering time will be coming up soon and he will need to know what to do for that. I will also need to find out if he knows anything about planting and harvesting the silo corn."

"Sounds like a good idea, but he will have a lot to learn." Sam said.

"I may have another good idea." Granny Edi said. "Abbi, didn't you say this Mrs. Granger was your housekeeper at one time?"

"Well, yes. And did a fantastic job of it. Why?"

"Do you think she would be equally as fantastic leading others? What I'm getting at is something I heard King and Russell talking about last week. It appears they have not had any luck hiring a Head of Housekeeping for the retirement home. Do you think your Mrs. Granger could handle that job, and would she want to follow in her nephew's footsteps and come work for the family?"

"Why, she just might! She was living with her sister up

until recently, but that lady died this past Spring. Since Mrs. Granger is now alone, she just might like to come here. I'll call her first thing tomorrow. "Now tell me all about the cave and tunnels. The short version, if you please. I need to get these two babies in bed soon."

They gave her and King a brief summary, with the promise of more stories later. Soon they were all headed for their bedrooms.

# Chapter Thirty-nine

"I HAVE FINISHED TAKING ALL THE pictures I need in the cave, Will. How long before you guys find out about the pressure washer?"

"Today, I hope. Now that you have pictures of the hole I fell through, King and I plan to put up the new door on this end of the main tunnel today. Then we can get started on the clean-up of the cave. Do you have enough light in the next part to continue with the picture taking?"

"Yes, and I am going over now. I would like to get all the pictures done before we leave for Copenhagen. That way, I can start putting my part of the book together if I have a few minutes of spare time over there. I shouldn't be too busy once we get to the dig, right?"

"Right. All they are asking of you is that you do a few nice shots at the site for their advertising brochure. The rest of the time, you can just relax, take the water taxi into town, travel around the Baltic, write your book, whatever you want to do. Look at it as a paid vacation."

"Whoopie! I'm liking this more and more. I don't like being away from the family, but this will only be a few months, and Sam will be here to help Granny cope with losing you again. I'm going now. Bye, see you at lunch."

And with a quick kiss to his cheek, she ran out the door, the saddlebags with her various cameras banging against her hip.

When she arrived at the cave she found everyone but Jeff, King, and Katie already there.

"I noticed all your horses were gone. What's happening here?"

Sam said, "The guys wanted to get ready to start the clean up as soon as we get the power washer and water truck in. Now that you are finished in here, they are stringing temporary wires to give us light to see the ceilings and walls. We also want to check very carefully to make sure we didn't miss any artifacts that need to be taken out before we start spraying water around. Did you notice anything when you were taking your pictures?"

"Well, yes. In addition to the old crates the journals were in, there are a few blankets on the bed ledges, but they are so rotten, I don't think there is any way to move them without having them fall into dust. I have several pictures of them, and when I told Will, he said about the only thing we can do is just trash them."

"Remind me to bring over trash bags the next time I come, along with some gloves. Anything I can do to help you?"

"Nope, but thanks for asking. I just plan to get a few shots along the length of the tunnels and several of that smaller cave in your mountain, then I'm finished! There are only so many pictures of the inside of a dimly lit tunnel that I can use! I need to get shots of the opening into the garage too, but that should take only a few minutes. See you back at the house."

"We will probably still be here when you come back this way, so I'll see you then."

"As a matter of fact, I'm not coming back this way at all. I walked through the pasture, and plan to work my way backward through the tunnels right into the furnace room. This portable lighting unit Russell fixed for me gives me just enough for my pictures and to keep me from being afraid of the darkness. This is the second day I have used it this way, and it works! Can you imagine the look on Will's face when I walk out of the tunnel and right into where he and King are working?"

"I think I will finish up here quickly so I can get back to see it! You just be careful in there by yourself. Don't do anything silly, like falling or getting lost."

"I'll be careful. See ya' soon."

Sam and her group finished all they could get done that day and returned to the house. Sam immediately went down to the basement. Will and King had completed the new door frame and had just put the new hinges on. As Sam walked over closer to them there was suddenly a loud moaning sound coming from the tunnel. She jumped, but moved closer, recognizing her friend's voice. The guys were staring at the tunnel entrance with a startled look on their faces.

"Have we woken up a ghost with all our noise?" King said.

"I don't believe in ghost, Will said, but it could be the wind blowing through the tunnel."

The moaning turned into a screech and came closer.

"What the devil IS that?" King said.

Suddenly, they heard loud pounding footsteps coming closer, and then Meli poked her head around the corner of the doorway.

"BOO!"

"Halloween is over, you crazy lady!" Will said and grabbed her to swing her around in a circle. "What the heck are you doing coming out that way?"

"Well, trying to scare you, for one thing. But most of all, to see if I had enough courage to come all the way through those tunnels by myself. I have only that small light, you know. But I needed to know if I could go that way to visit Sam and Jeff if I wanted to."

King came over and put his arms around her. He said; "I think that was a very brave thing to do, Meli. And just remember, by the time Sam and Jeff are in their new home, we will have those tunnels so well lit, you'll think you are on the sun porch upstairs."

Will whispered in her ear, "You don't have to prove anything to me, you know. You are very brave in other areas, and if you never get over your fear of the dark, it's fine with me."

She gave him a hug, then turned to Sam and said. "Did he look scared?"

"Well, maybe just a little bit! Hey, come on, let's get out of the way and let these guys finish putting that door on. Maybe it will keep out any other ghost that happens to be in there!"

Laughing and with their arms around each other, they headed for the elevator. Meli turned back to say, "Don't be long you two. Katie said she and Granny would have lunch ready about now, and I'm starved."

Over lunch, they all reported on their day, including the ghost in the basement.

Will said, "See! I told you those tunnels would be a fun place to play. I just wish I had known about them sooner."

Granny Edi turned to him and said, "You gave me enough gray hairs and worries as it was. Raising you with as few injuries as you had was no piece of cake, let me tell you! Swinging from the barn loft door, and you and Chris racing your ponies up and down that steep trail on the mountain. Sometimes I was thankful I COULDN'T see what you two were up to. And your Uncle Clifford covered for you more times than I can count!"

Russell said, "A little terror were you, Bro.? Seems not much has changed!"

# Chapter Forty

AFTER A FEW MORE TEASING jokes at Will's expense, they all separated to take care of their different projects in the afternoon. Granny Edi was knitting on the sun porch when Will came rushing in.

"Granny! Where is Melissa? I need to talk to her right away!"

"She said she was going down to her darkroom to get some of the tunnel pictures developed. What's wrong? You sound agitated."

"Everything. Nothing. I'll tell you later. I need to find Meli!" He rushed out of the room and she could hear him running toward the elevator to the basement.

He saw that the red light above the darkroom door was on, so he didn't dare open it and ruin Meli's pictures. He had to satisfy himself with pounding on the door and shouting for her to come out as soon as she could.

Ten minutes later Meli came out to find Will pacing up and down the new T.V. room. When he heard her come out, he ran over and pulled her into a bear hug.

"Guess what? I just got a call from the university in Copenhagen. They want me---us---to come over early. They want me to teach a short class to the volunteers before we go out to the island dig. Sort of letting them know what they will be getting themselves into and to recruit more if I think they will be needed. They are also putting me in charge of getting all the supplies needed at the site."

"Oh, Will, that is wonderful! How early is 'early'?"

"They would like to have us there by the end of this month, so the class can start on the 1st. Two weeks from today."

"Two weeks!"

"Can you be ready in that time? How far along are you with the developing? How about clothes?"

"Two weeks will give me just enough time to get all the developing finished. As to clothes, I'll pack lightly, then buy more there if I need them. But, TWO WEEKS! That doesn't give us much time with the family."

"I know, but they knew it was coming, and it's not like we will be gone very long. I estimate about six months at the most."

"You're right. Well, I guess we had better go tell the rest. Just let me shut down and clean up the darkroom."

They went directly out to the sun porch since they felt Granny Edi should be told first, and they knew it was going to be hard.

"I have had time to adjust to you two leaving, just not so soon. But Sam and Katie will look after me, so don't worry, I'll be fine. You will be able to call once in a while, won't you?"

"Sure thing. And I'll send you lots of postcards so Sam can describe them to you. Let's wait until after dinner to tell the others. Right now, Meli and I need to go to the office to make a few lists so we don't forget anything."

The after-dinner chat that evening was, of course, focused on Will and Meli's departure.

"Will said, "Even though I am looking forward to this job, I hate to leave with so much to be done with our new discoveries. Promise to keep me posted on the progress."

Sam said, "Well if you are like most men of my acquaintance, you will not miss the clean-up part at all!"

"Hummm. You may be right about that, but even that shouldn't be too bad with the use of the power washer. If it is delivered tomorrow as promised, maybe we can get that part finished before I have to leave. Then it will be just running the electric wires, and I'm not much good at that anyway."

"My wardrobe will need a going over, Sam." Meli said. "Can you help me with that like you used to do for my photojournalist trips?"

"Of course. As you well know, you will not need much more than jeans or shorts and tops. I don't think working on an archeologist dig will be much different than the photojournalist assignments you've been on. You will need a few nice things though, for when you tour the rest of the Baltic, as I know you will."

"Speaking of my other assignments reminds me." Meli said as she turned to Sam. "I guess I need to leave Cisco with you once more. The quarantine period for getting him into the country is almost as long as our whole stay will be! Then he would have to go through the same thing coming back. I would hate for him to go through all that if he could just stay here."

Surprisingly, it was Granny Edi who answered. "Of course he can stay here! Having you and Will gone is going to be sad enough, but I don't even want to THINK about not having my daily Hide and Seek game with that little scamp."

Abbi asked, "Is he still hiding your knitting bag, Granny? I thought he had given up on that."

"He still hides it, but that is the only thing I have noticed disappearing. I'm pretty certain he always puts my bag in the same place, but it is the fun of doing it that he likes."

Sam spoke up. "In case you haven't noticed, Granny Edi, I sometimes find it under the china cabinet when I am cleaning in here. I just vacuum under there and then put it back. You two enjoy the game so much, I don't want to spoil your fun."

"And I thought Prince was the spoiled one!" Katie said.

King chuckled at that, then turned to Will and Meli. "How are you getting to your dig? Isn't in on some remote island?"

Will answered, "Yes, about thirty miles offshore on one of the many lakes in the area. There will be a weekly supply run on a water-taxi from the city, but we will be pretty isolated most of the time. The island is not on a regular water taxi route, of course, but the university has made arrangements with one of the companies to bring out supplies and mail."

Meli added, "Being that far out should give me plenty of time to write all the captions for the tunnel photographs and get my part of our book completed. Will will have to write the historical narrative when we get back. Thank goodness, we do not have a deadline for this book."

"Just getting all of Meli's equipment and the photo copies for the book to Copenhagen is going to use up most of our luggage limit, but it will be worth the extra cost for overweight bags if she can finish our joint book and get a lot of good photos for her next one!"

"Say, listen, you guys." King said. "How would you like to travel there in the Mayhew-Cole Construction jet? I hear the architecture of the city is fabulous and is maybe something Russell and I need to study. Strictly research for future projects, you understand. It will be a longer flight, but there wouldn't be a weight limit on your luggage, and it would be much more fun than a commercial plane."

"That would be fantastic, King!" Will was at the edge of his seat. "It will save a lot of hassles in airports too. Meli refuses to check her cameras, so packs all of them in her carry-on. HEA--VY!! Especially if we come in at one gate and have to leave from another clear across the terminal."

Katie asked her brother, "What route would you take? There would have to be re-fueling stops."

"I haven't thought about that yet, but probably go up to Nova Scotia, then over to Greenland, maybe Iceland and Scotland if we have time, then directly into Copenhagen airport."

"King, we can't thank you enough." Meli said. "This will make leaving home so much easier. I was not looking forward to the trip over at all."

Abbi stood up and said, "Well, King, if that is all settled, we had better plan to start for home as soon as possible. We have to d-r-i-v-e the camper/trailer, you know. No quick trip with the plane!"

"Right! I had forgotten that little glitch in our timing. But if you guys have two weeks, I should have plenty of time to drive Abbi and the twins home, get the plane checked over, and get back here with days to spare."

# Chapter Forty-one

M ELI WAS GLUED TO THE window of the plane, busily snapping pictures, just as she had been for most of the flight.

"Better start stowing your cameras, Hun. We are about to touch down in Copenhagen."

"Just a couple more shots."

Will was packing up his own papers. He had been reviewing the letters from the University outlining what was expected of him. Since it was the third time he had done so, he figured he knew them pretty well.

They went through customs fairly quickly, hailed a taxi, and checked into the hotel where Meli and Will would be staying while he taught the class. King and Russell planned to start home the next week, giving themselves a few days to actually study some of the architecture of the city. After a short tour of the surrounding blocks that evening, they had dinner and returned to the hotel.

Will's course went well, with twenty students, six of whom would be working at the dig with him. Meli armed herself with city maps and went out touring every day, taking lots and lots of pictures. She sent postcards to the family, and thoroughly enjoyed the time.

Finishing up his lecture course, and checking to see that all the gear to go out to the site was on hand, Will spent a day talking to the people in charge of his dig. Then he and Meli headed for the island. They arrived about mid-morning and began setting up camp. As in all of Will's base camps, there was a tent for his (and now Meli's) use, one large tent for any artifacts found, and several smaller ones for his workers, plus the mess tent.

They had been at the site a little over two weeks when Meli announced she had finished her part of The Tunnel Book as she was calling it, and was now looking for something to keep her busy. She started taking pictures of the dig, the workers, the artifacts, the camp, anything she could find.

As luck would have it, a diversion arrived before she could get too bored. King, Russell, Katie, Susan, Will, and Sam had called to say they planned to come over for a vacation. They arrived in Copenhagen and settled into a hotel, having left Abbi and the twins to keep Granny Edi company.

Except for a short visit to greet the visitors and have dinner with them, Will had to stay at the dig, but Meli planned to stay with the others for the duration of their visit. They enjoyed a tour of Copenhagen, went to a lecture to learn about amber, and purchased several pieces of jewelry to take home. They took a ferry over to the wonderful Medieval town of Tallinn, Estonia for a day trip, then hired a car and drove all the way over to Bergen, Norway for a couple of days, visiting Oslo on the way.

When they got to Bergen, they decided it would be fun to hire a plane for an aerial tour of the glacier north of the city. The pilot and guide said, "Hello, and welcome to our tour service. My name is Anna. Just Anna. You could not pronounce my last name unless you speak fluent Russian. Please board the plane and we will be on our way."

As they all climbed aboard, King was looking the plane over carefully, noting that it had both wheels and retractable skis. Anna told him that it was the only way to be able to land the plane on ice or snow.

Soring over the beautiful mountains and fjords of Norway was breathtaking, and Meli was kept busy snapping pictures. Their guide was in the process of telling them about what they were seeing when her radio blared out a warning. The control tower back in Bergen was contacting them to give warning of a sudden out-of-season snow storm headed in their direction and advised them to turn around immediately.

Just as Anna started to turn the plane, she suddenly gasped and grabbed her chest, then slumped over the controls. Jeff was sitting in the seat next to her and reacted quickly.

"She's had a heart attack! Help me pull her off the controls! We're headed down!"

Jeff quickly opened her seatbelt and helped Russell lift her over the back of the seat and down to the floor.

King practically leaped over the seats and took over the controls. He scanned the gauges and began to bring the plane back to level. By the time he had done that, the sky was going from a beautiful blue to a very dark gray, and a few snowflakes were falling.

King said, "We're safe for now, folks. I just need a minute to figure out this control panel, and then I'll try to get us back to Bergen. How's the patient, Jeff?"

"Better. She had Nitroglycerin tablets in her pocket, so they helped. She is conscious, but not up to taking over the controls just yet! Not much more we can do for her until we can get her to a hospital. How are you ladies doing?"

Sam answered for all of them when she said, "As well as can be expected, I suppose. But I really don't like the looks of that sky!"

"Nor do I, Sis!" King said. "Can you guys find a way to secure our guide as well as yourselves? This may get to be a very bumpy ride."

Even as he spoke, a gust of wind hit the small plane and sent it listing to one side. The snow was coming down much harder, to the point they could barely see the ground below.

It kept getting worse, until finally, King said. "Listen, guys, while I am instrument rated, I have never flown through a snowstorm before. I really can't see a thing but I know there are mountains on every side. Before we slam into one of them, I think it would be best if I land this machine, and we wait out this storm on the ground."

They all agreed, so King started a slow, spiral decent until he could see the snow covered glacier just below them.

"Okay, folks, tighten those seatbelts, here we go!" King said as he pushed the nose down just a little more. Suddenly, they landed softly but immediately went into a spin. And kept spinning and skidding on the ice until they were suddenly brought up sharply against several trees at the edge of the glacier, then the plane tilted over until one wing rested on the ground.

In the silence as the plane stopped moving, they all heard the guide whisper something that sounded like "Forgot skis!" Then a bit stronger, "Get out! Tanks! Blow!"

King shouted, "God, she's right! We have to get out of the plane, NOW! Those gas tanks might have ruptured in the crash, and could explode any minute."

Even as he was talking, everyone was scrambling out of the doors into the howling storm. Jeff and Russell helped the guide manage the short distance to the ground, Katie had grabbed Susan in her car seat, Meli grabbing her cameras of course, and Sam grabbed Susan's diaper bag and the duffel that contained her food packets and extra formula.

Once they were all out of the plane, the guide again struggled to speak, "Get far away. Find big tree. Crawl under branches."

King set out, breaking a trail to a huge Norway Spruce about fifty yards from the plane. As the others came up to him, they pushed aside the lower branches that grew to the ground and crawled under. By crowding very close together among the bare spaces next to the trunk, they all got into the natural tent, and could no longer feel the wind or the snow on their faces. Just as they had all gotten inside, there was an explosion, followed by the sound of debris falling to the ground.

Anna groaned, but not from pain. She said, "There-goes-ride-home!"

Afraid the other tank would explode, King suggested they try to get as comfortable as possible right where they were until the wind died down. Anna told them to pull off a few branches that grew around them to sit on as it would be much warmer. The guys also pulled some branches to put under her and they all sat as close to her as the limited space would allow. Sharing their heat also benefited Susan. Katie had her in a tiny snow suit and a thick blanket over that, so was not too worried that she would get chilled, but appreciated the thoughtfulness of the others. Changing her diaper under these circumstances was a bit of a challenge, but Meli and Sam worked together and finally got it done. Once she was dry, Susan drank a full bottle of formula, then went to sleep.

Around the time sundown should have occurred, the wind began to sound less ominous. When King peered out between the branches, he reported that the snow had stopped and he could actually see a bit of sunshine on the treetops.

Then he ventured a suggestion. "If the second engine was going to explode it would have done so by now. I think all of us would be more comfortable inside the plane overnight, rather than under a tree where any wild animal might find us. I know I would feel much safer! Let's see if we can get back in."

King ventured out first, followed by Russell, then Jeff. They stomped their way to the plane and back to the tree several times to make a pathway for them to carry Anna. She was still conscious, but having severe pains in her chest, so Jeff did not want her trying to walk on her own. While Jeff and Russell made a 'seat' of their clasped hands and carried Anna back, King did a walk around of the plane to assess the damage. One engine was gone, of course, and the explosion had taken half that wing, both tires were flat, and part of the tail had been swept under a tree branch, so was broken off. He knew he could not get this plane back in the air, even with one good engine.

They all got back in and almost fell into the seats with gratitude, Anna actually sighing in relief as they placed her carefully on extra blankets made into a pallet on the floor. Sam and Meli had found several blankets stored in the baggage compartment, so each of them had one to throw around their shoulders. King went to the controls to see if he could get a message out but only picked up static.

As Katie started to give Susan her dinner, Russell looked over at her and said, "Well, Baby Girl, at least you won't starve while we are here! Sure wish I had something to eat!"

King was still fiddling with the radio, but turned to Russell and said, "Why don't you eat one of hers. As a matter of fact, if there are enough, we could all have a little dinner!"

Meli asked, "What are you talking about? You want us to eat baby food?"

"Why not? Katie, how many of those tubes do you have?"

"Lots! I just brought the whole bag instead of repacking some for this day-trip. Meli, Abbi told me about how easy it is to travel with babies these days. Just keep them warm, dry, and fed and they are wonderful travelers! The only problem is when we change altitude while flying, but a pacifier or bottle will most often change the pressure in their ears enough so they get over that fairly quickly. She also told me about these wonderful tubes of food. Susan is just old enough to start on food other than her formula, but packing lots of glass jars of baby food is not a great way to travel. These little tubes are great. They don't need refrigeration until you open them and it is all real organic food, processed so that babies can just suck it right out of the tube, or you can use a spoon."

"I've tasted them while I fed the twins and some of them are pretty good." King offered. "Do you have any with spinach, Katie?"

"Several, as a matter of fact. Here you go--apple, raspberry, spinach, and Greek yogurt. And I have pear and egg; peach, banana, and apricot; one called a Smoothie that is pear, sweet potato, and blueberry, with a little oats and white beans added, and a bunch of other ones. You guys look through the duffel and pick your buffet dinner. I have plenty of formula for Susan, so we don't have to keep any of these for her. At least, I hope we get back to where I can buy more pretty soon!"

"Let me have that tube that is just fruit for Anna, please." Jeff said. "That is probably all she should put on her stomach right now. How are you coming on getting a message through, King?"

"Not as well as I'd hoped, but I'll keep trying. The rest of you eat something, then try to get some sleep. It's been a rough day."

By that time, Meli was finishing up her tube of food and said to the group, "Well, it certainly isn't steak and potatoes, but isn't too bad. May I have a fruit one for dessert?"

After all of them had eaten their 'dinner', they tried to snuggle into the crazily tilted seats and get some sleep.

About midnight, King was startled awake by a voice coming over the radio. He had fallen into a doze draped over the controls, so his ear was almost on top of the speaker. It was the tower in Bergen looking for them. King answered quickly and gave them all the information he could about what had happened and his guess as to their location.

"Is anyone else hurt? Do you need emergency medical assistance?"

"No, nothing urgent. I told you about our pilot having a heart attack, but she is stable right now. However, she will need an ambulance standing by. How soon do you think you can send a rescue team?"

"As long as there is no emergency, we would like to wait until daylight before we send out our team. It will be easier to spot you that way. Look for them soon after you see the sun come up. Bergen out."

All but Susan had been roused by the talking, and sent up a cheer when they heard help would be with them soon. They began chatting happily but soon settled down to try to get a little more rest. Susan slept through it all.

Just after sunrise, they heard the whirr of helicopter blades and were soon back in Bergen, none the worse for their adventure. Jeff went to the hospital with Anna while the others went back to their hotel. When they all met for lunch, Jeff told them that Anna was going to be fine, just needing rest. King told them he had already talked with the tour company and found out that the plane he had wrecked was fully covered by insurance, and neither he nor Anna would be liable for the damages.

Katie said, "I think we should go by the hospital to see her before we leave town this afternoon."

They all agreed, and when they arrived in Anna's room they found her sitting up and enjoying an afternoon snack. She was very pleased that they had come to see her and asked them to sit and talk awhile.

Sam took the opportunity to ask a question that she had been thinking about since the accident. "Anna, getting us to crawl under that tree out of the storm was a very wonderful thing, and maybe even keep us from freezing to death. Whatever made you think about doing that?"

Anna smiled and said, "Didn't have to think. Have been doing it since childhood back in Russia. Almost everyone in my village has done it several times. When you ski a lot, to and from school every day, or just for fun, sometimes a storm will catch up with you, and you learn early how to protect yourself. One of my uncles had to stay under a tree for three days once. He was even able to light a small fire to help him stay warm and cook some food he had in his backpack. Using a tree for a tent is a common thing to do in these north country's."

They visited for another few minutes, then left to head back to Copenhagen where Will met them for a late dinner and an overnight stay.

Early the next morning, Will and Meli hopped on a water taxi and headed back to the dig site, while the others boarded their own plane and headed home.

# Chapter Forty-three

M ELI SLEPT IN THE NEXT morning, recovering from her fitful sleeping the several nights in Bergen. Finally getting up just after noon, she first went to the cook tent to see if there was anything to eat, then set out to find Will.

She found him on his hands and knees digging carefully into a small hole.

"What have you found, Hun?"

"Unfortunately, not much of anything, I'm afraid. Just a few pottery shards, just like every other artifact we have found on this cursed island. Broken!"

"Oops, guess this isn't a good time for you to chat. Why don't I go on back to the tent and get some of that film developed? See you later."

When Meli got back to camp, she set to work in the makeshift darkroom Will had put up for her in their tent. It was a very crowded space and not the ideal setup, but it worked. By using sheets of wood from packing cases their supplies came in, he was able to make a very small corner dark enough for her use. She knew she was 'behind the times' by still using film cameras, but she liked to do her own developing and trying different exposures and experiments on the negatives. She was using her digital camera more and more but still liked to play around with developing her own film.

In such a small space, progress was very slow and had taken weeks when she could have done it in days in her darkroom at home. She was only about two thirds through developing all the film from her trip around the Baltic with the others when Will came into the tent one evening and slumped onto his cot with a heavy sigh.

"What's the matter, Honey?" Meli asked as she came to sit beside him.

"I am just so discouraged! I was looking forward to this site so much because I had been told it had just been discovered, so I expected to find a great many artifacts. Do you realize how many we have found so far?"

Not waiting for an answer, he continued, "Including the three pottery shards the boys that discovered this place found, we have exactly twelve! Twelve! and every one of them broken! From what should have been a whole village of artifacts! We found the foundations where several lodges would have been, and we think we found the fire pit, but it's like someone else has been here and literally swept the place clean! What happened to everything? We have just about covered the whole island. There should be a pot or a bowl or a tool somewhere. We haven't found anything except the lodge sites to even indicate people ever lived here. I certainly can't claim this as a major site if my team comes up empty-handed."

"Oh, Will, I am so sorry things are turning out this way. Tell you what. King, Russell, and Abbi should be here tomorrow. King and Russel are coming to study more of the architecture in Copenhagen but why don't we ask them to come out here instead? You could take the whole day off, and we can show them around the island? You know, I have been wanting to climb up that big hill on the other side of the island. Maybe we could take some sandwiches and make it a day-trip."

"Great. I'm certainly ready to take a break. Maybe I can spot another potential dig site from up there. We may be digging in the wrong place!"

# Chapter Forty-four

"THIS VIEW IS FANTASTIC!" ABBI said as she turned in a complete circle. "It is so pretty. I wonder why no one lives here anymore."

"Probably because it is too far from things." Russell stated. "Even with the water-taxi that brought us out, it was a fairly long trip. Just think what it must have been way back before they had outboard motors to power their boats."

"Yes, you are probably right. Meli. MELI, come back! Please don't climb on that rock. It looks unstable."

"Don't worry, I am being careful. I just want a few more shots of this wonderful view. The water is almost like a mirror today. It makes a good pict…OH!"

"MELLISSA!" Will was running to her as fast as he could go, with the others right behind him.

"I'm okay, I'm okay, but I think it's my dignity that got damaged! Help me up, will you?"

"Here, take my hand, Meli." Abbi said.

"I have your cameras, Sis." Russell said.

"Come slowly this way." Will said.

"Ouch! That hurt! I think I may have twisted my ankle a little when I lost my balance on that rock. Just let me hold on to you for a few minutes. I'm sure it will be fine."

"Bring her over here off of those shifting rocks." King ordered.

"Sit down and let me take a look at it." Will said.

Carefully removing the hiking boot, he balanced Meli's foot on his knee. "That is definitely NOT fine, Meli!" he said as he pulled off her sock. Your ankle has already swollen to almost double the normal size."

Abbi knelt beside her and said, "It looks bad, old friend. You certainly can't walk on that foot. We probably can't even get your boot back on. How are we going to get her back to camp, guys?"

Will said, "You three stay here with her while I hike back and pick up one of the all terrain vehicles. This hill is sloped enough; I think I can get it right up the side if I take it slowly. It will be a bumpy ride back for you, Meli, but it's the quickest way."

Abbi, King, and Russell made Meli as comfortable as possible, then settled down to wait.

Meli wanted them to talk to her to keep her mind off of the pain in her ankle, so kept asking questions about the people back home.

"I thought Granny was planning to come with you on this trip. What happened?"

Abbi laughed, then said, "She suddenly remembered there was a meeting of the church Fall Bazaar Committee that she just had to attend. You know her fear of flying. I don't think we will ever get her up in a plane!"

"Hello, the hill!" They heard the shout about five minutes later. Will parked his vehicle as close to Meli as he could, then he and Russell gently lifted her in. Abbi climbed in beside her and put Meli's leg over her own lap to pad the bumps as best she could. Russell and King said they would hike back, so Will turned around and headed back to camp.

"That is too cold!"

"Quit complaining, Meli. You know you have to keep it on that ankle. Just be glad there was still some ice in the chest."

Will turned to the others and said, "I really hate to cut your visit short, guys, but I would like to get my cranky wife back to the city and have a doctor take a look at this ankle. I'm afraid she may have broken it."

"I agree." Russell said. "Let us collect the things we dropped in your tent, and we can all take the water-taxi on his return trip. Good thing he is still here."

King said, "I'll go and see if I can help get those supplies off-loaded. That may speed things up a bit."

Within fifteen minutes they were headed for Copenhagen as fast as the taxi captain could push his craft.

At the university clinic, a young doctor came to them and said that Meli's ankle was broken, but not too badly. They were getting ready to put a cast on.

"However, I do have a question about her blood work. I would like to keep her here long enough to run a couple of different tests. Nothing to worry about." He was out the door before they could ask any questions.

He came back shortly and asked which of the gentlemen was Meli's husband. Taking Will into the hall, he asked, "Did you or your wife know that she is pregnant?"

When the other three heard Will's shouted "WHAT!" they all came running into the hall.

"We're pregnant!" Will told them, then whispered it over and over, as if it would not sink in.

Later in her hospital room, Will was pacing and stopped in front of her to say, "All right, Mrs. Melissa Brackston, I'll say this one more time. King is taking you home. Period. No arguments."

"But, Will, I…"

"No arguments. You can complain all you like, but think about it. You have taken a gazillion pictures, both at the dig site and here in town, AND in all those other places you went, so you don't need any more. You can not help me at the dig with a cast on your foot, you have finished work on our combined book, and are starting on another of pictures of this area, which you can work on at home."

"He's right, Sis." King said. "The sooner you get home so Jeff can oversee your health, the better it will be. For you AND the baby."

"But all my gear and cloths are still out at the dig."

Will said, "Got it covered. Abbi and I are going to hire a motorboat and have them take us out to the camp. While I am packing up your camera equipment and film she will pack your clothes and the Tunnel Book materials. We should be back here by dinner."

Russell said, "I am to stay here and badger you until they get back. King is already headed out to the airport to have the plane checked over, then as soon as we have you and your gear loaded, we will head West. You can be in your own bed by tomorrow this time, with Granny, Sam, and my Katie to cater to you. Katie is going to be so happy when she hears about the baby. Our Susan will have a playmate very close to her own age!"

"Oh, all right. I'll go, but I'll miss you, Will."

"Hey, if we don't find something to show the university soon, this dig will be canceled, and I may be home a lot sooner than we thought. In any case, it's only a few weeks more. There's Abbi now. Were you able to get a boat, Abbi?"

"Yes, and he is all gassed up and ready to go. We are to meet him at the dock in five minutes, so get a move on."

# Chapter Forty-five

J EFF AND SAM WERE THERE to meet the plane when
it landed, with Katie right behind them with her car.
Because Russell was the first off the plane, he was almost
knocked over when Katie threw herself at him.

"Hey, slow down! It has only been three days since I
left. Where is Susan?"

"Molly Evans is watching her. Molly has been so great
helping with the twins while Abbi was with you and
King. Right now she has all three!"

"Oh, Meli, how do you get yourself in so much
trouble?" Sam asked as soon as they had helped her out
of the plane.

"You can fuss at her later, Love. Right now, we need
to get her into the back seat of my car and get her home.
Anyone else riding with me?"

Abbi said, "You go on and get Meli in bed. I'll help tie
the plane down, get the rest of our luggage, and ride back
with Katie. Meli, all of your cameras are here in Jeff's car
as well as your clothes. We will be right behind you."

On arrival at the farmhouse Meli said, "I will **not** go
up to bed! I'd miss all the gossip that way. I want to stay

right here on the sofa, then when the rest of the family gets here, we can have a nice chat and catch up."

Doc Simmons had been notified of Meli's ankle and the very good news of the expected baby so he came by that night. Molly Evans decided to stay to hear all the news. She had watched all three babies while Sam and Katie were at the airport. Now with both mothers taking care of their own children, she was free to just listen. It was a noisy, happy group, but they didn't stay together long. Most of them were just too tired.

Meli stayed off her foot for two whole days before she couldn't take the inactivity any longer. She took the cane Doc had brought over, grabbed her cameras and undeveloped film from her office and went down to the darkroom to finally develop the last rolls of film.

When she came back up, she had a puzzled look on her face. She found Sam and Granny knitting on the sun porch and said, "Sam, take a look at these photographs and tell me what you see."

Sam looked closely at the four pictures, then said, "Well, these were obviously taken on that last day, from the top of the hill. The huge expanse of water around the island is very impressive, but what are these? She pointed to two darker images at the bottom of the pictures."

"What do they look like to you." Meli asked.

"Well, I know it sounds crazy, but they look like ship shadows in the water. Shadows of two large ships."

"Ah-ha! I knew it! I believe that is exactly what they

are. Not shadows precisely, but the outlines of two sunken ships. Do you know what this means? These ''shadows' may hold the artifacts Will has been searching for all this time. I've got to call him right away, never mind the time difference."

"You have GOT to be kidding!" Will said. Meli's call had roused him from a sound sleep, so he wasn't sure he had heard her correctly. "Send one on your phone right away, then fax the rest. Turn the setting to 'darker' so it will show the image better. If you are correct, these may be why there is nothing here. It was all being moved away with the last inhabitants of the island! They didn't get very far because they were most likely horribly overloaded. There were probably no survivors to tell anyone about it because most people of the time could not swim."

As soon as the picture on his phone showed up, Will knew Meli was right. When the faxes came in, he looked at the photographs closely for a long time and came to the same conclusion Sam and Meli had seen. These were ship's shadows, and could possibly be the key to why he had not found anything at his dig. As soon as it was daylight, he called his boss at the university and told him about the pictures. Later that same day, a large boat with lots of sonar equipment came to the island. Using the landmarks in the photographs, they went to the approximate location and started searching the bottom of the lake.

Sure enough, they located what was left of two very old sailing ships.

Divers and a team of archeologist that deal with shipwrecks were called in, and they started salvaging a multitude of artifacts from those ships. It seems they were indeed full of people. Whole families, who were moving to someplace else, so they were carrying all they owned with them. There was nothing left on the island to find.

Will was still in charge of the dig even though it had now moved to the water, and he even got a chance to put on a wet suit and go down with the team several times. When they had brought up as many artifacts as they could find, and he had cataloged all of them at the university, he caught a commercial flight home.

In the family room that evening, he said, "Because the ships were in fresh water, they were not damaged by all the worms and things found in salt water, and because the water is always very cold in that area, it acted as a preservative. All the artifacts are still in pretty good shape. The people at the University there are ecstatic about this find because of the lost history it represents.

"And, on a personal note, the best part is that I get full credit for the 'find', which will boost my credit standing with the university here when I apply for that professorship I want. AND my lovely wife will receive a co-owners claim to the site for her contribution. If she had not taken the photos from the top of that hill, the ships may never have been found."

# Chapter Forty-six

"**N**ow, back to our very own family and what they have been doing. Russell told me that Jude arrived and is working out very well. What about his aunt. Is she now in charge of Housekeeping at the Home?

King said, "Yes, she was happy to come and work for us. If you remember, my wonderful wife gave her a trust fund, so she really doesn't need to work anymore. However, with her sister gone and Jude working here, she was lonely. She was happy to come take the job with no salary, just room and board!"

Russell spoke up to say, "Actually, she is now living in Si and Jenny's old apartment. They bought a lot from Amy and built a house of their own right beside her. Joel and Calvin are very happy about that, as are Jenny and Amy. They have become close friends. Also, Jenny has rented one of the old meeting rooms from us. She has turned it into a small flower shop so the residents can purchase fresh flowers or birthday balloons, and she puts small bud vases on all the tables in the dining room. It all seems to be working out well."

Sam turned to Russell and said, "I would like to talk to you about that, Russell. Building a house of their own,

I mean. Now that Meli and Will are back, do you think we can get started on the new house for Jeff and me? Just the garage and my advertising business office at first. My new car needs a roof over her head, and if I can move my office out of your old 'tool shed' apartment, Joel could live there rather than in your guest room. It worked for you for what? Four years? So he should be comfortable in those rooms too."

"Well, I don't see why not." Russel said. "But Jeff tells me you guys have changed your minds about using the tunnels for living space. Is that right?"

"Yes, and that is why I said just the garage for right now. We talked about using the tunnels and caves, but neither of us felt comfortable with it. All those beautiful natural formations! We just don't feel right taking a chance of maybe damaging them. We would like to incorporate the Crystal Cave somehow, and my little pond, but no actual living quarters inside the mountain. But that means King will have to change our plans and I know that will take time. But the garage with my office on the second floor was always going to be outside just at the base of the mountain anyway, so those plans will not have to be changed. I would still like the main house to be connected to the tunnels somehow, but not with living spaces, just a passageway of some kind."

"You know what? Since King and I are very much into commercial spaces now, why don't we contact Si and see if he would like to tackle a private home this far from the lake? If he will, he probably could get it done sooner than I could anyway."

"Super! Will you call him? Or should Jeff?"

"I'll call tomorrow. I can probably explain what you want better than you could."

"What do you mean?"

"I think what my bumbling husband is trying to say, is that he can speak 'home builder talk' better than someone not in the construction business." Katie said. "Now, may I have another piece of that peach pie before we get back to Will's questions?"

After more pie all around, Will settled back and picked up where he had left the conversation earlier.

"Okay, to continue! I hear the cave cleaned up very well, so what is next. Lighting the tunnels?"

"No, no, no." Sam exclaimed.

"Why shouldn't they be next?" Will asked.

"No tunnel lights yet!" Sam said. "Well, in the main cave, yes. But not in the tunnels yet, except for just enough light to see what we are doing. Every inch of those tunnels needs a good vacuuming to rid them of years of spider webs and dirt. That is a chore we have been putting off because it isn't a pleasant one."

"But the guys have been busy in and around the cave." Katie said. "We have put a gate in the fence and cleared all the brush from there to the cave. Even Granny Edi could go, with a little help over the rough spots. We have turned those ledges the first generations were using as beds into sort of 'buffet' ledges. They will make a very nice place to put the food for our picnics instead of tables taking up floor space. And guess what! There is even a bathroom! Well, not really, but King showed Russell how to put a chemical toilet in that little alcove where we found the ledgers."

Sam added, "Russell has added a permanent generator so there is power for lighting or cooking pots, and he even added one of the heating units like these in the house. We can now have family gatherings even in the winter!"

Granny Edi spoke up to say, "And the most amazing thing! You know how wet it always was back there. Well, the boys have re-routed a couple of the springs into a sort of cistern affair, so there is running water inside the cave. And that is drying out a lot of the land. We might even be able to walk on it now without sinking in the mud!"

Abbi said, "So we really don't have to wait for the tunnels to have lights! We can have a family gathering there any time. Let's throw a party!"

## The End

Note to readers: The idea for the ship shadows in this novel came—in part—from the story of The VASA. A 64-gun warship that capsized and sank 1 hour into her maiden voyage in 1628, this magnificent ship stayed on the bottom of the harbor in Stockholm, Sweden for over 300 years. The VASA now resides, fully restored, in her own museum in Stockholm.

CPSIA information can be obtained
at www.ICGtesting.com
Printed in the USA
BVHW031610010419
544230BV00004BA/298/P